The Juan les-Pins Affair

Glenn C. Smith

Copyright © 2006 by Glenn C. Smith

ISBN 0-7414-3357-5

Published by:

PUBLISHING.COM

1094 New DeHaven Street, Suite 100
West Conshohocken, PA 19428-2713
Info@buybooksontheweb.com
www.buybooksontheweb.com
Toll-free (877) BUY BOOK
Local Phone (610) 941-9999
Fax (610) 941-9959

Printed in the United States of America

Printed on Recycled Paper

Published June 2006

Other books by the author

Tybee Island Terror Plot, 2001

Golden Lily, 2004

The Juan les-Pins Affair

Introduction

Money Laundering is an illegal method of shifting money acquired from criminal activities into legitimate businesses. As huge sums of dirty money are recycled daily, the ring of corruption can capture politicians, regulators, entire government agencies and financial institutions.

Money Laundering is a crime. Some analysts say that this activity may be the third largest industry in the world.

Perhaps the most highly visible money laundering case to come to light in 2003 was the United Nations administered relief effort for the Iraq people called the Oil for Food program. The Wall Street Journal and ABC NEWS have reported widely on this story. U. S. officials say there is solid evidence that Saddam Hussein diverted at least $20 billion to his personal bank accounts in Europe by skimming money from the Oil for Food program.

After the invasion of Iraq, it was discovered that Saddam Hussein had insisted on extensive record keeping of the names of politicians, corporate executives and shadow corporations that received secret oil allocations from the Iraqi Oil Ministry. These records have been used by investigators to expose corruption at the highest levels of the United Nations and governments of European countries.

This is a fictional story about how one person became a whistle blower and helped the American CIA track down a bank in France that was used by Saddam Hussein as a depository for his laundered assets. French and Russian crime syndicates were involved with Saddam's banking operation which had a base in Juan les-Pins.

This action adventure story takes place six months before the American invasion of Iraq. Saddam Hussein has attained his pinnacle of power. The United Nations Oil for Food Program has given Hussein a golden opportunity to engage in kickbacks, bribery and corruption.

The Juan les-Pins Affair

Prologue

"Captain Ghadi, sir, the port authority at Marseilles has ordered that we change our ETA at the oil refinery dock to 1300 hours," said the First Mate. Ghadi frowned and wondered why the port authority had issued new orders.

"Very well, alert the First Lieutenant and Cargo officer about the new ETA," said Ghadi.

Ghadi knew full well his cargo bill of lading papers were cleverly falsified to commingle smuggled oil with his legitimate 1.8 million barrels. The change of arrival time orders was an unnecessary reminder that his tanker was carrying smuggled oil. As he looked through the windows on the bridge, muscles in his neck and face tightened with tension. Had an informant tipped the French port authority officials about his oil smuggling? Would there be extra inspectors to certify his oil tonnage? He told himself to relax, remain calm and not make too much of the new ETA.

"The First Lieutenant and Cargo Officer acknowledge our new ETA," said the First Mate.

"Very well," answered Ghadi as he worked to get back in control of his mind. No need to get upset, he said to himself.

Ghadi had been a ship master for ten years, learning his trade by working up through the ranks of merchant shippers around the world. He had observed that most of his former captains engaged in small time smuggling on the side to augment their income. Drugs, weapons, stolen cars and luxury merchandise were commonly stowed inside containers that were then carefully hidden aboard the huge tankers. The smuggled goods were almost always off loaded from the big ships at night after the legitimate cargo.

Pumping extra oil aboard the tanker, a technique called "topping-off," after the legitimate cargo had been loaded, was the simplest method of smuggling. A few adjustments to the logs made no cargo inspector the wiser. A well placed bribe to a port inspector and nothing would be said. If by chance a challenge was made about the cargo, a Captain and his officers could plead ignorance.

With this change in his ETA at Marseilles, Ghadi now had six hours to kill before the harbor pilot came aboard to guide his tanker into its berth at the oil refinery pier.

"Slow speed to five knots," ordered Ghadi. This barely kept headway on the tanker, but he decided this was the best way to kill time. If the Basra Queen dropped anchor the ship might be easily boarded by port security forces for another inspection. This he did not want. After ordering the slower speed, Ghadi decided to retire to his underway quarters directly behind the bridge to again check the bill of lading. Before leaving the bridge, Ghadi glanced at the instruments readings, scanning the radar for any ships on a collision course. He noticed nothing unusual. In short, all was well on the bridge.

"I'm going to my quarters. Take over the conn but let me know of any ship contacts appear on the radar that would require us to steer a new heading."

"Aye, aye, sir," said the First Mate.

Ghadi had been the Captain of the Basra Queen since the huge tanker had been purchased by AMEP (African Middle East Petroleum Co., Ltd.) two years ago. He had been recommended by two Iraqi ship captains who were aligned with the Baathist Party in Baghdad. His First Mate, Hoshyar al-Sadr, had served with him on his previous command. Each man understood about merchant ship masters smuggling contraband for personal profit. Neither man confided in the other about their small private schemes, but this oil topping-off activity was so huge the two men cooperated fully in every detail. This was the third voyage that Ghadi and Hoshyar al-Sadr had participated in an oil topping-off operation.

After clearing French port authorities at Marseilles and the security inspections, the Basra Queen began the process of unloading her oil. The process was complicated, requiring almost two full days. Once the off loading of the oil cargo began, all crew members not directly involved were given liberty.

At approximately 1800 hours, a port authority security van rolled along the pier next to the tanker and stopped at the forward brow gangway. Two well dressed men stepped from the van and climbed the catwalk to board the tanker. The two men headed directly to the Ghadi's quarters. There was no need for an escort because they had visited Ghadi aboard the Basra Queen on previous voyages to Marseilles. The first man was a short overweight Russian. The other was a lanky but muscular Frenchman who had worked all his life on the Marseilles docks. Both were armed with pistols which were holstered underneath their suit coats. Ghadi was expecting them and welcomed them to his cabin.

"My paperwork is in order and the ship has passed port authority inspection by the security forces. Our unloading process continues on schedule. We will be done in thirty-six hours," said Ghadi.

"Yes, it would appear so," said the overweight Russian with a snarl on his face. He motioned to the Frenchman with his hand and pointed toward Ghadi's desk. The Frenchman carefully placed a briefcase on Ghadi's desk and backed away.

"Your payment, Captain, for bringing the oil cargo to us without problems," said the Russian.

Ghadi looked at the briefcase and placed his hand on the smooth black leather top. He didn't speak but nodded and smiled at the Russian.

"You may count the money, Captain," said the Russian.

"No need to count it. I'm sure it's the correct amount."

"Then our business is done?"

"Yes, it would seem so," said Ghadi.

"All right then, until next time," said the Russian who got up, turned with the Frenchman, and left Ghadi's cabin and walked off the ship.

Ghadi unobtrusively watched the two French mobsters leave his ship and drive away in their van. Once he was certain the visitors had gone, he picked up the ship's telephone to ask the First Mate to come to his cabin. While waiting, Ghadi counted out the First Mate's share of the smuggling pay-off and put it on the desk. He placed the black briefcase containing the rest of the pay-off money underneath his desk. A knock at the door announced the arrival of the First Mate.

"Come in."

Upon entering Ghadi's quarters the First Mate's eyes immediately fell upon the money piled upon the desk.

"Fast payment makes loyal fast friends. This is your cut for our topping-off deal. I trust you won't spend it all in one place," said Ghadi with a smile.

"No, sir, this money goes into a special bank account for my retirement."

"A wise move, although you must spend some of this money on wine and women, don't you?" asked Ghadi with a smile.

"Rarely. May I ask, Captain, what do you consider is a good use for this money?"

"Commercial real estate in Paris. I like small office buildings and apartment houses downtown."

"Sounds like a wise investment," said the First Mate.

"Cash is too dangerous in this world economy. One day the Euro is strong the next it is weak. Interest rates are too low. I want cash-flow and some hedge on inflation," said the Captain.

"Perhaps, I too should begin this type of investing," said the First Mate as he saluted Ghadi. He left the cabin with the money jammed in his pockets.

*　　　　　*　　　　　*

After the fall of communism, many Russians left the Soviet Union and drifted to the Cote d' Azur seeking a better life style. The Russians brought their bureaucratic skills and latent entrepreneurial talent. Increasingly, their skill and talent were put to quick use to organize powerful underworld cartels. If the Russian gangsters weren't able to buy into a French crime syndicate they used force to take over the operation. Many of the Russian immigrates had no respect for international law. Their only interest was making money. The Oil for Food Program administrated by the UN for the relief and benefit of the Iraqi people fit perfectly into their crime mode.

Many Russians had long standing contacts with Saddam Hussein and his oil ministry. Iraqis in the oil ministry found it easy to fake oil tanker cargo loading so their Russian crime syndicate partners in France could skim off profits. Kick-backs to Saddam followed every smuggling operation. Oil allocations were used to placate important officials in France, Russia and various European capitals.

*　　　　　*　　　　　*

The Russian mobster, Viktor Belov, and his French assistant, Henri Dupre, studied the paperwork while seated at a corner table of a bistro in the la Madrague section of Marseilles.

"When will we be able to pick up the oil receipts from the refinery manager's office?" asked Dupre.

"Only after the cargo of oil has been pumped from the Basra Queen into the tank farm and the delivery is certified by the oil storage loading manager," answered the Russian Belov, without raising his eyes to look at Dupre, he continued to examine the paper work and bill of lading. He knew the oil refinery loading manager took bribes to accept a greater amount of oil than was specified on the tanker's bill of lading. The refinery loading manager would order the extra oil to be pumped into a special segregated holding tank, certify its quantity, then hold it for sale by commodity brokers into the international oil market. The price of oil had been fluctuating wildly on the London commodity exchange due to unrest in the Middle East.

The following day the oil receipts were picked up by the Russian Belov and hand delivered to the Commodity Exchange Offices in Marseilles. This was his routine. There was never a suspicion that his activity was tied to Saddam Hussein's Oil for Food relief program.

The receipts were logged into the AMEP account and readied for sale. The account in Marseilles was controlled by Munir Abdelnour, an executive of AMEP. Several days later the oil contracts were sold during a rally in the international oil market. The AMEP account was credited with Euro cash receipts for subsequent distribution to various French politicians in Paris and Marseilles. Detailed records of the sale of oil and check distribution were sent secretly to the Iraqi Oil Ministry in Baghdad.

The Juan les-Pins Affair

1

Tankaji Ushiba, underworld boss of the powerful Japanese Yamaguchi Gumi in San Francisco, sat calmly in his office sipping warm sake from a favorite demitasse cup. The number two man of the Yamaguchi Gumi, Osami Muto, looked at his boss and said,

"The intelligence we received about the CIA officer is reliable and worth acting upon. I believe we can easily eliminate him in his room at the Fairmont Hotel. If all goes well, his body will not be found for several hours after our man has done his work."

Ushiba sat quietly reflecting upon what his second in command had said. He again tasted the sake, paused, and spoke in a quiet voice.

"What is our back-up plan if there are problems killing this CIA officer at the Fairmont Hotel?"

Muto was prepared for this question because he knew that Ushiba was never satisfied with just one plan. Ushiba always wanted a contingency plan.

"Our best female agent made contact with the officer last night at the Top of the Mark. She managed to arrange a dinner date with him for this evening if our man fails his assignment at the Fairmont."

"Excellent. You have done well. We cannot afford to fail with this contract against such an important target. Our organization will lose face in Tokyo if we do not complete this contract. Go ahead with your plan and keep me informed."

*　　　　*　　　　*

McQuesten checked his Rolex and wondered how much longer the meeting would drag-on. After three days of speeches, presentations and endless commentary about money laundering, the conference had become tiresome.

McQuesten had an eight o'clock dinner reservation at Garibaldis on Presidio with a lovely lady he had met the night before. Kitty Cook had said she was an interior designer for the in-crowd around town. McQuesten had her phone number and debated whether to call and reconfirm his date.

McQuesten was staying at the Fairmount Hotel across from the Mark Hopkins on Russian Hill. He thought his room acceptable but a little staid. The Hay-Adams Hotel in Washington, DC, off Lafayette Park would always be his favorite. There was something the Hay-Adams had that made him feel comfortable and well cared for. The last meeting of the conference adjourned and the audience headed to a private lounge for refreshments.

McQuesten's boss, George Tilghman, had sent McQuesten to this San Francisco conference as a little perk to get him away from the pressure of Langley.

McQuesten remembered the conversations well,

"Jack, there's a conference in San Francisco I want you to attend. It will be a no-brainer for you. It will give you a chance to loosen up and relax in a great city. Also, I don't want you concerned over writing any reports after you get back. You need to see how the other half of the world lives. Not quite a vacation, but close enough."

Tilghman thought that San Francisco would be the perfect city for McQuesten to relax and unwind. Tilghman had always told his officers it was important to learn how to relax. This had been his routine now for two days; however, McQuesten noticed the attendees of the conference thinned out after each day.

On this last day, McQuesten would have one scotch and soda for appearances, then go to his room, and get ready for the evening with Ms. Cook. As he finished his drink, he noticed an oriental man near the door eye-balling him.

McQuesten tried not to appear alarmed but he didn't remember seeing this man in the conference meetings.

McQuesten walked back to the bar, returned his empty glass, dropped a tip on the plate, smiled at the bar maid and turned to look at the door. The oriental man had disappeared and wasn't anywhere in the reception lounge area. At this moment McQuesten's internal alarm senses kicked-in. He subconsciously moved his arm against the side of his body to feel his holstered pistol. His weapon of choice was a Beretta .40 caliber model 96F, matte blue finish, three dot sights with a ten round magazine clip. After another quick visual check for his oriental friend, he walked toward the door. There was something McQuesten didn't like about the way the stranger looked. McQuesten felt that he was being lined up in the cross hairs of a sniper rifle scope.

McQuesten got to the elevator and waited for the doors to open. He casually looked around the crowd. There was his new friend, stalling around at the back of the crowd waiting to get on the elevator. The doors of the elevator opened and McQuesten faked a move toward the doors but then side-stepped his way to the stairwell. McQuesten figured he could climb up a flight of stairs and order another elevator from the mezzanine.

McQuesten opened the stairwell door and ran up half the way, turned around and waited to see if his tail followed. The door below opened and the oriental guy moved into the stairwell. He looked up, spotted McQuesten, drew out a pistol equipped with a silencer and took aim at McQuesten. He squeezed off two shots that missed. McQuesten pulled his Beretta pistol and fired once down the stairs at his attacker.

McQuesten then raced up the stairs to the next level and found the door locked or held closed by someone on the other side. McQuesten turned again toward the pursuer and was ready to shoot again. The assailant was lining up his pistol for a shot but was hurting because McQuesten had scored a hit with his shot. Before the man could fire again, he dropped to the stairs and his gun fell from his hand.

McQuesten slowly walked down the steps to the man and asked,

"Why are you trying to kill me?"

The man struggled to speak but whispered, "I'm under contract to kill you." And then he went limp and breathed his last. McQuesten checked the man's pockets and found a small wallet with a photo ID California driver's license. His name was Kaji Ugake, 1708 Fillmore Street, San Francisco. Obviously, a hired hit man paid to kill. "Most contract killers don't carry ID cards in their pockets," thought McQuesten as he wiped his finger prints from the ID and replaced it in the man's pocket. McQuesten thought again, "This must be his first job, or else he was very confident about doing his chosen profession."

Since no one came to investigate all the commotion, McQuesten continued up the next flight of stairs and walked to the elevators. He went up to his eighth floor room, carefully entered, and bolted the door behind him. After searching the room for signs of illegal entry, he got out of his clothes, showered and readied himself for his dinner date. "Just another day at the shop," thought McQuesten as he wondered to himself, "Who wants me dead and why?"

About the time McQuesten was ready to leave for Garibaldis restaurant the room telephone rang.

"Yes."

"Jack, this is Sally at headquarters. Please drop everything and get back as soon as possible. Something big has come up in Europe and we need you there. The next flight home is eleven o'clock local time. You have been booked with a first-class ticket and have pre-boarding clearance at the diplomatic security check-in gate."

"Sounds good, I'll have dinner and go directly to the airport. Anything else you can tell me about Europe?" asked McQuesten.

"Yes, but it will have to wait until you get back to Company headquarters. Have a good flight. See you soon."

As McQuesten put down the receiver, he looked out the room window at the park below. There were little kids being walked around by nannies and others playing with dogs. Very normal, just what one would expect to see in the warm late afternoon sun.

McQuesten picked up the city telephone directory and looked for Kitty Cook to check the number and her address in the city. He found her number with a street address – 1708 Fillmore Avenue – the exact same address he found on the ID of the dead hit-man. A little man inside his head began waving a red flag. McQuesten went into his defensive mode and decided to dial her number. If she was working with the hit man she might be somewhat surprised to hear his voice.

Before dialing he tried hard to recall how he had met Kitty Cook at the Top of the Mark. He had been sitting alone at the bar looking out the windows at the city below. Kitty Cook had apparently approached him from his right side sinse he didn't see her walking toward him from the front of the bar. She nudged him and said, "Hi there, mind if I join you for a drink?" As McQuesten turned around to see who was talking, he noticed she was a smashing brunette about five-nine and filled out in the right places.

"Sure, glad to have some company. My name is McQuesten, Jack McQuesten. Who are you?"

She looked him straight in the eye and said,

"I'm Kitty Cook."

"Well, Miss Cook, please let me buy you a drink. What will it be?" asked McQuesten.

"I'll have a Stinger," said Cook as she then said, "Please call me Kitty."

It wasn't too long before they were engaged in conversation.

"Do you come here often?" asked McQuesten.

"It's one of my favorite places. I keep hoping to see Cary Grant and Suzy Parker come to the bar and order Stingers like they did in that old movie," said Kitty.

"Oh, yes. I do remember that scene. Grant was a navy pilot back from the Pacific war doing some war bond rally work to energize the home front, I believe. Something like that," said McQuesten.

"What brings you to San Francisco, Jack?" asked Kitty as she cocked her eyebrow and waited for his answer.

"I'm here on a conference about international banking," said McQuesten.

"Sounds awfully dull," said Kitty.

"You got that right," answered McQuesten.

"Will you be in town for long?" asked Kitty as she probed a little further about McQuesten.

McQuesten remembered he thought Cook was an experienced talker and knew just when to come in with the right question. Her timing was good. McQuesten was starting to get his guard up, but her classic appearance was over-riding his concerns about whom she might be working for. He went along with her routine.

"How about dinner tomorrow night?" asked Cook, again, smiling and looking into his eyes.

"Well, I suppose that could be worked out," said McQuesten as he thought to himself, "I wonder if this woman wants me to make a pass at her tonight or keep me waiting until tomorrow.

"Sure, why not. How about eight o'clock at Garibaldis, on Presidio Street," replied McQuesten.

"Sounds like a nice place. I've seen it but never been there," said Cook as she wrote her telephone number on the back of a book of matches.

"Here's my number. Call me anytime if there's a problem with tomorrow. I have to go now, but thanks for the drink," said Cook.

At least this is how McQuesten remembered things.

He dialed the number.

"Jack, it's nice to hear your voice. Are we still on for dinner tonight?" she asked in a calm voice. A little too calm for McQuesten's comfort, he thought to himself.

"Yes, I'm looking forward to seeing you," said McQuesten.

"Why don't you come over to my place for a quick cocktail before we go to the restaurant?" asked Ms. Cook.

"I don't think so. I've got to clean up a few things and there's just not enough time. It's very nice of you to offer. Let's just meet at the restaurant," said McQuesten.

"That's fine. See you there," said Ms. Cook.

McQuesten put down the phone and thought what she had said. This broad is a great actress but he was on to her.

McQuesten packed his bag carefully and made sure there was one round in the chamber of his pistol. He slid his Beretta into his shoulder holster and hung it on the back of the chair. He then went to the bathroom to freshen up one more time.

After going through the express check-out procedure, McQuesten walked outside to the curb and looked for a cab to take him to the restaurant. As he stood by the curbside he heard a feminine voice, "Jack, over here!" McQuesten looked and saw Kitty Cook leaning out of a cab window. "Come on over. We can ride together to Garibaldis."

McQuesten looked and saw nothing suspicious that got his internal alarms going so he headed for her cab.

"My goodness, what a nice surprise. What's this all about?" asked McQuesten.

"Oh, I just thought it would be fun to ride together," said Cook.

McQuesten glanced at the cab driver and thought he looked out of place driving a cab. He seemed too well groomed and not wearing the usual ruffled up clothes of a real cabby. McQuesten tossed his single piece of luggage onto the front seat, opened the back seat door, and climbed in the back with Ms. Cook.

As they rolled along the busy streets engaging in small talk, McQuesten happened to notice another cab coming up along side. It was too close to his door and window. He looked over and saw a Japanese guy pointing a gun with a silencer directly at him. McQuesten instinctively dropped down as two bullets whizzed over his head. The driver of his cab yelled,

"Hey, stupid, look what you've done. You've hit the lady."

McQuesten looked toward Ms. Cook; she was slumped against the opposite cab door. The other cabby made a quick right turn and raced down a side street. McQuesten looked at his cab driver; he had pulled a gun and was lining up for a shot. McQuesten kicked the back of the driver's seat with his foot and ruined the driver's aim. His shot went wild, shattering the back window glass into a thousand pieces.

McQuesten pulled his Beretta and squeezed the trigger twice, firing two slugs through the back of the driver's seat. The driver slumped forward; the cab lurched to the right and jumped the low curb. The cab rolled down the side walk about twenty feet before slamming into a street lamp pole. Fortunately, no pedestrians were walking along the side walk. An old pan-handler who happened by walked up to the cab window and said, "What's going on here?"

McQuesten gathered himself, got out of the cab, retrieved his luggage from the front seat and said to the pan-handler, "I don't know, but they're not well."

No police came along to investigate what happened so McQuesten nonchalantly walked up the street until he found another taxi parked in front of a cheap hotel. The driver was asleep at the wheel. McQuesten knocked on the window with his Columbia University ring and said,

"I need a ride to the International airport. Can you take me?"

"Sure, get in. It'll cost you twenty bucks," said the cabby.

"Not a problem. I'm in a hurry, let's get going," said McQuesten.

As his taxi moved along in traffic McQuesten heard some emergency vehicles headed back to where he had left the other cab. McQuesten looked the other way when the police cars passed his cab.

After checking his Beretta pistol and luggage through the security gate, McQuesten headed for the first class passenger lounge. He chose a seat in the corner away from the other passengers. He carefully looked at each passenger as they entered the lounge hoping that none of them was thinking of using him as target practice.

It would be good to leave this city. He wondered how he'd compose his report about the two Japanese who attempted to kill him. Tilghman would certainly ask why one of his officers was the target of two well planned assassination attempts. McQuesten heard his flight being called away. He finished his drink, picked up his newspaper and walked to the gate.

The Juan les-Pins Affair

2

The return flight from the West Coast left McQuesten feeling irritable. Jet lag, too much alcohol and bad airline food combined to get the morning off to a bad start. As he was slowly getting into his morning routine, the telephone rang. McQuesten took a deep breathe and exhaled before picking up the receiver.

"McQuesten."

"Jack, Tilghman here. Come to my office at the Old Executive Office building at 1100 today. We need to talk about an important assignment in Western Europe. We'll have lunch and you'll be back at headquarters by 1430." The tenor of Tilghman's voice was serious. McQuesten sensed this new assignment wasn't to be a cakewalk through the capitals of Europe.

"Thank you, see you at 1100," said McQuesten as he waited for his boss to hang-up. It wasn't good form to hang up until you heard your boss say good-bye or the line go dead. He began to clean up old paper work and looked over his desk calendar. He decided nothing was urgent, just the routine stuff he could handled later. Lunch in D.C. sounded great. It would be a step up from the routine institutional food service at headquarters.

McQuesten decided to drive to the White House compound. He always felt uncomfortable being shuttled around Washington like a diplomat. Besides, his black XJ6 Jaguar needed to show the other cars on the road it was the big cat.

McQuesten leaned back once more into his desk chair, stretched out his legs and propped his feet up on the corner of the desk. As he dug back into the Wall Street

Journal, out of the corner of his eye he noticed the telephone button was flashing. Just then his assistant, Miss Sally, spoke over the intercom. "There is an FBI agent named Paul Holder, calling from Charlotte, holding on your line. He was the officer-in-charge a year ago when they arrested Sergei Bruslov."

"Oh yes, I remember. He's a good man."

McQuesten folded up his paper, tossed it into the basket and reached for the phone.

"Hello, agent Holder. What can I do for you?"

"Captain, this is agent Paul Holder. I've got news about Sergei Bruslov, but I'm afraid it's bad news."

"I thought Bruslov was in the Federal slammer."

"You're partially correct. The last eighteen months he has been in Federal custody at the lower New York District jail in Manhattan, on 26 Federal Street awaiting the outcome of an appeal after his terrorist conviction. He somehow managed to hire a Russian attorney from Brighton Beach who did a good job representing him. After losing his appeal, he was scheduled for transfer to a Federal prison in up state New York. However, in the transportation process, the prison van broke down on the Thruway. Three Russian mobsters following the van overpowered the marshals and freed Bruslov. Now he's at large. We have no clue how these Russians pulled this caper off. Our best guess is that Bruslov has crossed the Canadian border and probably is on his way to Europe."

"My God, how did this happen? I can't imagine such a breakdown in security."

"I agree. The episode stinks. We can only speculate, but someone sabotaged the prison van in the jail garage so it would breakdown on the way to the Federal prison," said Holder.

McQuesten did a quick recall in his mind about how Bruslov had double-crossed the al-Qaeda team in Savannah just before their dirty bomb was to explode. Somehow Bruslov eluded the Arab terrorists and got as far as Charlotte before the FBI captured him. The al-Qaeda ring decided that

Bruslov had caused the failure of their mission to blow up Savannah, GA.

"I'm sure that if the al-Qaeda cell in London gets the word that Bruslov is back they will track him down and cut him into little pieces," said McQuesten.

"That's for sure," agreed Holder.

"Thanks for posting me on this. I'll put a note in our file that Bruslov escaped." For all the good it will do, thought McQuesten.

"I thought you should know what happened. The incident took place twenty-four hours ago," said Holder as his voice paused, waiting for any further reaction from McQuesten. Finally, McQuesten spoke up, saying,

"If there is further news on Bruslov let me know."

"Not a problem. If we get news, I'll pass it along to you."

McQuesten hung up his phone, turned his head toward his window and stared at the trees in the background thinking, "Now there's another guy out there gunning for me."

At ten minutes to 1100 McQuesten was driving through the White House gates. After obtaining his security clearance at the White House appointment gate, he walked across the West Executive Avenue and entered the Old Executive Office Building. He made his way to the elevators that would take him up to Tilghman's fourth floor office. He made it a habit to pause for a few moments on the main floor to look at the black and white marble floor that had been laid during the Civil War. He often thought about the many Generals, Admirals and Secretaries of State that had walked on this marble floor. General U. S. Grant and President Lincoln could easily have walked along these same marble panels. After a few moments of reflection, McQuesten made his way to Tilghman's office.

Tilghman's office was comfortable, roomy with plenty of space to relax, but still it maintained an aura of business. After their greetings, Tilghman, seemingly in a reflective mood, as he sat behind his desk opened up with a soliloquy musing about the folklore of covert action during the days of the Cold War. Tilghman began by saying,

"General William, 'Wild Bill' Donovan of OSS fame during WW II finally convinced the Truman Administration to close down the OSS in October 1945. Ultimately the CIA was born in 1947. By then the US realized that the Soviet Union was our main threat and the Cold War began in earnest. In 1955 a joint British/American operation was undertaken with great secrecy in Berlin. A tunnel was dug from the American sector into the Russian sector of Berlin and wire taps were placed on Soviet military telephone lines. With this CIA/MI6 operation in place, the volume of raw intelligence developed was so voluminous that the analysts were hard pressed to cope with the traffic. After millions of dollars were expended on the Berlin tunnel, the operation was blown to the Russians by a Soviet agent who worked in the British Planning Committee executive. Upon learning that the tunnel operation had been blown to the Soviets by a British operative, the CIA was never sure that they could work effectively again with MI6 or MI5. This opened up all sorts of possible scenarios about Soviet moles in the British intelligence service. By 1965 the CIA was convinced that the British service was riddled with Soviet moles. James Angleton, Chief of Counterintelligence at Langley, flew to London to discuss this issue. The Brits listened but said little. Angleton left London thinking the Brits felt the CIA should look for dust in their own closets. Maybe I should slow down. Pretty soon I'll be talking about code breaking and the Venona files."

Tilghman paused, sipped his cup of hot tea, and said, "For some reason, I seem to be anxious to unload this on you morning. I hope you don't mind listening to all my rambling. Well, let's get down to business. I want to go over some points about the Patriot Act of 2001."

McQuesten reacted, saying,

"I enjoy listening to your thoughts about what went on years ago with the CIA. It puts things into perspective. Thanks for telling me about them."

Tilghman switched gears:

"The Patriot Act of 2001 grants us wider authority than ever before to pursue terrorists and their activities. Title Three of the Act allows us more running room to track down money laundering activities in this country plus we can now follow up leads developed here that take us into the European banking system. Our station chief in Copenhagen received a tip from a Danish citizen who suspected that his bank was involved in a money laundering ring that started with deposits from Pakistan and ended up in France. We don't know yet if this tip is legitimate or maybe a sting operation set up by the crime syndicate. These rings are cautious and suspicious. They continually test their members to see if someone might be leaking information to Interpol or state security forces."

McQuesten listened to his boss. He knew when to come in with questions about where he would fit into the operation. He always marveled at Tilghman's prodigious memory and mastery of the English language in his conversations. To McQuesten's way of thinking, it was no wonder that Tilghman had such a big job in the CIA. As he sat listening he reminded himself, "Listen to the whole story then ask your questions."

"By tomorrow this time you'll be in Copenhagen getting the local picture from our station chief. His name is Brad Ramsey. He's a good man who worked in the Middle East before taking over in Copenhagen. I think you'll get along well with him," said Tilghman.

"As you now see things shaping up, what will my role be in Europe? To whom will I report while I'm there?" asked McQuesten.

"You'll work alone most of the time but run things through Ramsey while in Copenhagen. He'll plug us in on whatever you develop. After Denmark we'll have to play it by ear. You can contact me directly or back through headquarters," said Tilghman as he leaned forward with his elbows on his desk and fussed with a paper clip.

"Let's go to lunch. We can discuss a few more things at the La Maison Blanc. Their special today is grilled grouper. My secretary checked out the menu for us," said Tilghman.

"I'm ready," said McQuesten.

Tilghman and McQuesten walked out of the Old Executive Office, through the White House appointment gate and crossed Seventeenth Street. They proceeded down the tree lined street to F Street and into a large white marble façade building that was the home of the restaurant, La Maison Blanc. The maitre d' greeted Tilghman and led them to a corner table. As they walked through the dining room McQuesten recognized several ex-senators seated at tables engaged in talk with Administration officials. The white walls were covered with large prints of soldiers and horses in Civil War battle dress fighting over a hill in Virginia. All the windows were draped with white see through linen. Soft classical background music by Faure filled the room. A waiter hovered near-by the table to bring them ice water and warmed rolls with sweet smooth butter. They both ordered the luncheon special, grilled grouper.

Tilghman lowered his voice and began the conversation by saying, "I've ordered our satellites to be over Denmark and France on a special reconnaissance schedule that will allow you access 24/7 to communicate with our man in Copenhagen or back here to Langley. Your cell phone will be powered with new special cadmium batteries that will provide all the power you need for the next six weeks. We will supply you with an up-graded cell phone masking code. That should cover your communication needs as long as you're on this assignment. You'll have official cover and be working initially through our embassy in Copenhagen. Our man Ramsey will set up your contacts with the French intelligence services: The General Directorate for External Security (DGSE) and Counter-Espionage Service (DST). He will also coordinate your movements with Interpol in Lyons. We will give Ramsey power to arrange air transportation for you if needed to get you in and out of any tight spot where your mission may take you. Usually air transportation must be coordinated through the Embassy however, this assignment is too important to be hung up on that administrative requirement."

"I appreciate hearing this. Sounds like you've thought about everything."

The rest of the lunch went smoothly. After coffee the two men took several extra moments to stroll through Lafayette Park back to the White House.

After saying their goodbyes, McQuesten drove his XJ6 through the traffic with more resolve. He headed home to pack his bags and get his house set for an extended absence. His cleaning lady, Mae, had a key and she stayed to her schedule. If he wasn't around, she knew the drill: clean the house and check the fridge for leftovers. Whatever looked interesting, she was welcome to take home. She fed the cats and then left them on their own.

McQuesten's big problem was always what clothes to pack for his assignment. From what he'd been told he probably wouldn't be hiking in the woods or climbing over rugged mountains. The job sounded like conservative sportswear was in order and a few dark sweaters. Perhaps a pair of his favorite Armani sports shoes and loafers for dinner. He picked out one conservative blue silk tie and a light blue button down casual cotton shirt. He decided to wear a blue blazer and gray slacks on the flight to Copenhagen. He packed several expensive golfing shirts and two crew neck white long sleeve pullovers plus underwear and socks. If he needed to add something to his traveling wardrobe his policy was always to purchase it at decent men's clothing store.

McQuesten arrived at Dulles International airport at 1600, checked through security and headed for the first class passenger lounge. He was able to breeze through the security check-points since he was traveling with a diplomatic passport. His Beretta model 96F .40 caliper pistol and extra ammunition clips was sealed in a special Company approved traveling case and placed in his checked luggage. McQuesten reviewed the departure board for the SAS flight 912 scheduled to depart at 1840 and arrive in Copenhagen at 0810 the following morning. He hoped that all the first class passengers would be tall, blonde good-looking single Danish ladies.

After ordering his favorite Cutty Sark and soda from the bar, he sat down in a comfortable chair in the first class passenger lounge. To kill time he decided to read another unclassified memo from Tilghman that summarized the US concerns over money laundering as perceived by the Financial Action Task Force (FATF) established by the G-7 in Paris in 1989.

Currently, there are twenty-nine countries that are members of the FATF. In 1999 it was estimated that money laundering amounted to 1.5 Trillion dollars annually. This amount of money is the equivalent to the value of the total output of an economy the size of Spain.

Money laundering processes criminal proceeds to disguise their illegal origins. The obvious sources of funds that must be laundered are from illegal arms sales, drug trafficking and smuggling by organized crime operations. The scale of these networks is unimaginable to the honest commercial banking corporations.

McQuesten's SAS flight was finally called for boarding. As he settled back into his seat for the eight hour flight to Copenhagen he scoped out the females in first class. He decided none was going to rev up his libido.

He nursed his glass of Merlot through the plane's take-off as it climbed up to its cruising altitude. Closing his eyes, he let his mind roll back to his Tin Can destroyer duty days as an OOD conning the ship hunting for submarines in the north Atlantic. McQuesten loved his destroyer duty and always felt at home conning the new ship.

*   *   *

The Spruance Class destroyer bridge was twenty-five feet across and twelve feet fore to aft. Outside of the enclosed bridge the bridge wings afforded the OOD clear view of the entire five hundred sixty three feet of the ship. Ltjg McQuesten was familiar with every square foot of the bridge and the purpose of all its equipment. He could find his way around the bridge blind-folded. He stood at the front window staring down at the bow as it plowed through a heavy sea. The Bridge communicator broke the silence,

"Sir, we have a sonar contact bearing ninety degrees relative. Range four thousand yards," shouted the sonar operator.

"Very well, Helmsman. Right full rudder. Come up on course zero-four-five," ordered McQuesten.

"Zero-four-five, aye! Rudder is right full. Coming to zero-four-five," answered the helmsman.

"All engines ahead two-thirds. Make revolutions for twenty-five knots," ordered McQuesten.

"Sonar, this is the Officer of the Deck. Keep me advised on this contact."

"Aye, aye, Bridge," answered the Sonar operator.

"ASROC mount, this is the Officer of the Deck. Advise your status."

"Sir, ASROC mount is manned and ready. All rockets locked on safety mode awaiting orders to release safety locks."

"ASROC mount, this is the OOD. Check and continue to maintain safety mode on all weapons."

McQuesten could still remember the vibrations in his shoes as the destroyer picked up speed. The four gas turbine engines were capable of developing twenty thousand horsepower each to drive the ship in excess of thirty knots. The marine jet engines labored as the engine shafts cranked out more revolutions to the twin screws. The white foam behind the stern kicked up and left a wide beautiful trail. The Captain looked at McQuesten from his chair on the bridge and said,

"Mister McQuesten, I'm going to let you run this entire drill. I'll be here for any questions, but I will not help you get out of any jam. This is your drill to screw up or handle properly. I'll be sitting here in my chair evaluating how you conduct this drill. When McQuesten reached this part of his reverie he always dozed off.

*   *   *

Miss Sophie Goodbody was seated at her desk staring out the office window at the Vallens Bank funds transfer unit in downtown Copenhagen. The recent news of her brother's death in the terrorist train bombing in Madrid had shaken her deeply. She finally gathered herself and looked back at the work on her desk.

Goodbody and her younger brother grew up in Randers, Denmark. Five years separated the two children. Her father was a Master of a large ferry ship that regularly ran from Copenhagen to Oslo carrying cars, trucks and tourists. Sophie's mother remained home to raise the children since their father was away due to his work.

After the children had graduated from middle school she became a hotel chef.

As a young school girl beauty Goodbody was regarded as an attractive favorite of all her male classmates. Now, at twenty-eight she had taken on movie star looks that turned heads everywhere she went. Her mouth had beautifully formed thin lips that projected a friendly smile with perfectly configured white teeth. Many said she reminded them of Grace Kelly or Alexis Smith.

Goodbody completed three years of higher education at the university but finally tired of attending classes. She had several romances but never married. A Danish Air Force officer she loved dearly lost his life in an airplane accident during NATO maneuvers. After his death, Goodbody found it difficult to become seriously involved with anyone else.

Goodbody worked at the Vallens Bank for six years and enjoyed her independence. She never gave up hope that one day she would settle down and raise a family. She enjoyed sports. Standing five feet nine inches, she had an athletic tennis game and also lifted six pound weights regularly to tone her muscles.

While handling the daily work routine at her desk, she had begun to question the huge amounts of money she was sending over the wire system to other banks after being held overnight in her bank. The office manager had reminded everyone to send along the funds according to the instructions and not question where the money originated. Goodbody knew that these large amounts of money didn't originate from within their Danish banking operations or any Vallens Bank European branches. She suspected something was fishy.

Goodbody had a mind for numbers and she easily memorized the special account numbers used everyday to send along the huge transactions. She had prepared a journal notebook at her apartment which was not far from the bank office. She tested herself every night to see if she remembered the account numbers correctly. She never made a mistake entering the numbers into her diary.

The banking institutions in Europe that weren't recognized by even the most seasoned senior bank colleagues were the easiest for Goodbody to remember. Bank manuals had to be consulted to determine where the new banking clients were domiciled.

As the daily funds transfers continued to grow larger, Goodbody began asking herself, did the department heads at headquarters know about all the money being routed through this satellite office? Worse yet, did they even care? That was the real question that needed to be answered.

Goodbody's office workmate girl friend spoke to her and broke her day-dreaming,

"Sophie, shall we have lunch together and get some sun?" asked Bridgette Tofte.

"No, I brought lunch from home. I'm going to eat alone in the park. Thanks for asking though," said Sophie.

After finding a quiet bench near the water fountain, Goodbody opened the morning paper to the business section. Her eyes came across an article by a local feature writer dealing with terrorist funding rackets, specifically, money laundering. Goodbody became transfixed by this article.

It was like reading a report right out of her office. The only thing not mentioned, was the name of her bank. The last paragraph mentioned that the offices of Interpol and the American FBI were aggressively involved in the hunt to find and smash these funding schemes of terrorists.

That evening Goodbody was alone in her apartment listening to her favorite classical music station. Her mind drifted back to the newspaper story. As she read the article again, she thought perhaps an officer at the American Embassy might be interested in her banking journal information. Goodbody thought that someone in the law enforcement business would know if her suspicions were correct or off base. She made up her mind. She would not continue to sit on this information she had collected. The suspicions had built up in her mind were bothering her. It was now time for her to act. She would get her answers about the bank's money transferring operation. Tomorrow at lunch she would call the American Embassy. She picked up her telephone book and memorized the phone number.

*   *   *

"American Embassy. How may I assist you?"

Goodbody hesitated. She caught her breath and said,

"Yes, I'd like to speak to someone about bank money laundering." It felt strange hearing herself say the words she had read in the newspaper. The next voice she heard was masculine and deep and belonged to a man who sounded very official.

"Brad Ramsey here. What can I do for you?"

"Yes, I work in a bank here in Copenhagen. I read the article about money laundering in yesterday's paper. Are you familiar with it?"

Ramsey paused and said, "Yes. I read it carefully. Would you please identify yourself."

Goodbody paused and said, "I'd rather not give you my real name for security reasons. Let's just say for now, this is Vera Woodsen."

"All right, Ms. Woodsen, what can I do for you?"

"I believe I may have information that relates to bank money laundering, but I'm not sure. I don't want to cause a problem for myself, or my employer. You see I'm not sure how to handle this concern of mine," said Goodbody.

"Tell me what you have on your mind," Ramsey said.

"No. Not over the telephone. We must meet somewhere in a public place where we can talk without drawing attention," said Goodbody.

"That's fine. Tell me where and when you want to meet for coffee or lunch," said Ramsey.

"There is a small sidewalk café on the Stroget about two blocks past the Kongens Nytorv, on the north side of Stroget. I'll be there tomorrow about twelve thirty reading a book. Next to my coffee will be my small red purse. How will I know you?" asked Goodbody.

"Okay, I'll be wearing a light brown sport coat with an American flag pin on the right lapel. I'm six foot two inches with dark brown hair. I'll carry a newspaper in my left hand. How about if I ask to join you since all the good tables are taken? said Ramsey.

"Everything is fine, except no American flag pin. That's too obvious. Wear a Denmark flag pin in your lapel," said Goodbody as she paused to add, "If one of my office buddies happens to be at the cafe, I'll say no, get up and leave. You follow me to another sidewalk café along the Stroget."

"Okay, until then tomorrow at the café. May I add that you are very professional and cautious," said Ramsey.

"I've read lots of spy novels and I'm nervous about our meeting," answered Goodbody.

That evening sleep didn't come easily for Goodbody. Her telephone conversation with the man named Ramsey was still on her mind. She tossed and turned in her bed for hours as her mind second guessed her motives. Why hadn't she asked someone in her bank management about her concerns? Why had she decided to contact an outside agency about her suspicions? She finally decided that the newspaper article had tipped her over the line to call the American Embassy. Also, her suppressed feelings about the new female supervisor from Paris weren't positive. This woman wasn't like other management women Goodbody had worked under at the bank – so cool and detached from the office staff. Goodbody knew she wouldn't fall asleep until her mind sorted out all the questions and resolved the issues. She struggled to find answers so she could settle her mind and go to sleep.

*   *   *

Brad Ramsey was the only child in the family that lived in the northern Detroit suburbs. His father was a mechanical engineer from the University of Michigan. He was now the chief designer at an automotive technical center in the northwest suburbs. His mother was a co-owner of a fashion boutique that catered to the wives of automotive executives and their children.

During the summer vacation of his junior year in high school Ramsey was coming home after playing baseball. He noticed his father's car in the driveway and wondered why his dad had come home so early. Ramsey's mother met him at the door,

"We just received news that Uncle Charlie has been killed in a flight training accident in California. He's taking it terribly hard. There's nothing we can do for him at the moment."

Ramsey's uncle had graduated from the US Naval Academy and was a fighter pilot. He was killed during a training mission off the California coast practicing carrier qualification landings piloting an LTV F-8U Crusader jet.

After the news of his brother's death, his father was despondent for several months. Ramsey decided to apply for the naval academy and this decision gave the family a huge psychological lift. Ramsey was nominated to the academy, gained his acceptance, and graduated in the top ten percent of his class. Upon being commissioned he was ordered to destroyer duty for four years. After completing his tour of sea duty, he resigned from the Navy and joined the CIA.

*   *   *

The next morning Goodbody continued to be apprehensive over her meeting with Ramsey. She was tired from her restless night. Her face wasn't relaxed. She appeared tired as she stood in front of her apartment mirror applying her makeup. She decided to drink a second cup of coffee to help clear up her mind. She looked forward to the walk to work in the fresh air along the Stroget thinking it would help calm her nerves.

Again, she turned down a luncheon invitation from a co-worker, saying she wanted to eat alone and finish reading a book. No one seemed to question her decision. She had picked out a conservative blue dress and tossed a white cotton sweater over her shoulders. At the last moment, she slipped on a pair of tan leather walking shoes. As she left her office for lunch, Goodbody checked behind to see if any nosey girl friends were tagging along behind to see if she was meeting a new boyfriend. They weren't visible as she turned to walk along the Stroget. Crowds of shoppers were packed together as it was a warm day with plenty of sunshine. Goodbody easily found a table near the outside window that provided some security from eavesdroppers who might wonder what she and her companion were saying.

"Mind if I join you?" asked the tall, handsome American. Goodbody looked up and was happy to see a good-looking man who undoubtedly could pull off this meeting without causing a scene. Goodbody thought they looked like any other couple having a romantic luncheon. Goodbody gave Ramsey a nod that said fine, please sit down and get comfortable.

"Miss Woodsen, if you still prefer that name, please tell me how I may help you."

"Woodsen will have to do for now," Goodbody said as she took a breath and said, "I'd like to see some real identification."

"Not a problem," as Ramsey reached into his jacket pocket and snapped open a wallet with his picture ID card. Goodbody looked closely at the ID card. It had US Department of State written all over it. Goodbody felt a thrilling sensation go through her body as she thought, "Oh my God, I'm meeting the US State Department." As Ramsey put his ID back in his pocket, Goodbody thought she caught a glimpse of a shoulder holster and pistol tucked under his coat jacket.

"What can I do for you Miss Woodsen?" asked Ramsey.

Goodbody took a deep breath to compose herself as best she could. She looked into the eyes of Ramsey and liked what she saw. Somehow she felt she could trust him. At this point what was she going to do, get up and run back to her office?

"I work in the funds transfer office of a large bank. We have branches all over Europe with offices in London and New York City. I work in a satellite office with a group of ten people, mostly women, who send wire transfers of funds around the world to settle security purchases, large corporate purchases of heavy equipment and commodities, mostly crude oil. I've noticed lately that our branch has become involved in handling huge sums of money, in dollar denominations, that originate in Pakistan and flow through the European System Central Banks (ESCB) system to our bank. This normally wouldn't be a problem except, with the funds from Pakistan, there isn't any listing of what the money is settling, like fuel or commodities, or the like. Do you understand what I'm saying?"

"Yes, I think so. Have you ever gone to your supervisor and asked about the lack of supporting data for the money being sent through your office?" asked Ramsey.

"My supervisor is new to her position. She came to us from Paris. She knows the business but she's very cool. Not easy to approach with problems. I don't trust her."

Ramsey looked at Goodbody for a moment and tried to digest what he was hearing. Goodbody thought he was getting ready to ask questions. She didn't know it of course, but he was having a hard time concentrating on the business at hand, while sitting with such an attractive woman. She hoped she could answer any questions he might ask her. While there was a momentary pause, she looked around to see if she recognized any of the sidewalk café patrons. Her coffee was getting cold. She signaled the waiter to bring more to the table.

"When the new supervisor started to work did you notice an increase in the funds coming from Pakistan?" asked Ramsey.

"Yes, come to think of it. After she showed up the volume of funds transferring from Pakistan without the normal supporting documents did pick-up."

"Is this woman married? Does she have someone she sees on the weekends? Have you ever seen her in a social situation around Copenhagen? Like a museum or theater, something like that?"

Before Goodbody could answer any of his questions, he asked again, "Do you think she lives alone or with someone?"

Goodbody wasn't ready for all these questions from a stranger she had just met. She didn't feel that comfortable opening up to this Embassy person no matter how handsome he was. She began to stall with her answers and tried to think about his questions. Finally, Goodbody blurted out, "It wouldn't surprise me if she was a lesbian. She is masculine with hard facial features. Not soft with some femininity. Also, her clothing wardrobe is obviously not important. I'm just guessing of course, but that's what I'd say, off the top of my head."

Ramsey looked at Goodbody for a moment. He finished his coffee, took a breath, and said, "Okay, enough about her. Do you have any names of people that might lead us to an organization that is moving these undocumented funds around Europe?"

Goodbody looked at Ramsey but held back. This is going too fast for the first meeting in a sidewalk café she thought. "Maybe later, I can show you all that I have," said Goodbody.

Ramsey thought about that offer but gathered himself and then got back to business. Perhaps this woman is going to try and hold out for money for her information. "I can't promise any compensation for what you pass along to me. I'm also wondering why you contacted us. What's your motivation?" Ramsey purposely held his breathe and looked squarely into her eyes waiting for her answer his question.

"I can assure you it isn't money. My brother was killed in the Madrid railroad bombing. If terrorists used my bank as a conduit to pass along their funds, I'd like to help you nail them, if it's possible. Of course, I know that my information may not be connected with the bombing in Spain. There is however, a chance they may be one in the same. That is my motivation. Does this make any sense? Or, are you thinking that I'm a little female nut-case who shouldn't be taken seriously?"

"No, no. I don't think you're strange in any way. Your concern about the bank being used as a conduit is excellent information. However, before we go our separate ways, let's agree how I can contact you and where we should meet. I don't think I should call you at your bank office," said Ramsey.

"Yes, I agree with you. I'll contact you and please remember, my name is Vera Woodsen," said Goodbody.

"In case someone is watching, I'm going to slip one of my cards under your purse. When you leave make sure you have it. You can call the number and ask for me anytime, day or night, 24/7. If I don't answer someone will take your message. I'll get back to you if you leave a number where you can be reached," said Ramsey.

"Good. Let's leave it that way. I must be getting back to work. Thank you for meeting me today," said Goodbody. Ramsey smiled, casually got up to leave and said, "Pas paa," and then he disappeared into the strolling crowd.

As Goodbody sat alone for several moments at the table she could only think of this man's US State Department ID. Also, the pistol under his coat did not make her feel comfortable. She wondered if she would again have trouble sleeping tonight however, it was a nice gesture by him to pay the bill. As Goodbody walked back to work she began to feel better about her decision to contact the Americans.

*   *   *

Headquarters for Interpol was in Lyon, France, however Interpol had established their money laundering task force unit in Paris. One of the Paris office branches in specialized in recruiting computer hackers who were trained to track down money laundering activities within the European System Central Banks. Money laundering was roughly defined as any act to conceal the identity of illegally obtained proceeds so that they appear to have originated from legitimate sources. The Paris Interpol computer geeks weren't above technically attacking a bank if they possessed solid evidence that the bank held deposits illegally obtained from kick-back artists and under-the-table schemes utilized by the likes of Saddam Hussein.

After receiving information from banking regulators, the American FBI or employees from European banks the Interpol hacker group began its attack on a target bank's security system. Usually the Interpol money laundering task force hackers could retrace the routes used by the money laundering rings. Recovery of money from scams isn't part of the Interpol mission, however recovered money deemed to be dirty can be used as evidence by Interpol prosecutors against organized criminal activity.

Currency laws are enforced if broken by criminals who are engaged in financial and high tech crimes. The European Banking Federation (EBF) will assist Interpol money laundering task forces by making use of its Anti money-Laundering International Database (AMLID). By pooling information and tips from bank employees, the EBF and Interpol have busted many illegal money laundering rings operating in Europe.

The Juan les-Pins Affair

3

McQuesten retrieved his single piece of brown luggage at the bag rack reserved for travelers carrying diplomatic passports. The airport security agents paid him scant attention as he walked up to the customs window, received a passport stamp of approval and moved along in the crowd. As he stopped at the luggage inspection tables, an agent tied a bright red and white tag on his bag handle and waved him through the lines. The narrow aisles in the airport were more functional than what he was used to in the States.

McQuesten was soon walking on the curb outside of the airport looking for transportation to the Plaza Hotel on Bernstorffsgade. The air was refreshingly cooler than the humid atmosphere of Washington, DC. He calculated there were almost sixteen degrees of latitude difference from Washington, DC and Copenhagen. A well groomed young man dressed in a dark suit approached him and asked quietly,

"Are you Mr. Jack McQuesten?"

McQuesten looked over the man and decided he seemed fairly normal. "I could be - who wants to know?"

"Sir, I'm from the American Embassy. Mr. Ramsey sent me to pick you up and take you to the Plaza Hotel." McQuesten stood steady for a few moments and then said, "Okay, but I have to see some ID before I get into your limousine."

The young man produced his diplomatic ID card and a Danish driver's license. It all seemed legitimate so McQuesten climbed in the back seat of the limousine.

They drove through the Copenhagen traffic and were soon at the Plaza Hotel, which was across the street from the old railroad station building. Crowds of people walked through the station doors coming and going to the trains. Bicycles of every description were parked in racks near the station doors. The special bike traffic lanes were full of well dressed bikers moving along together. Taxis lined up along the curb outside the Plaza Hotel waiting for business.

Once in his room, McQuesten went through his usual routine of checking the room for electronic bugs or any listening devices. He carried a CIA issued electronic gizmo hidden inside an electric razor that could detect any type of listening bug implanted in his room walls, TV, radio or telephone. Satisfied that all was kosher, McQuesten unpacked and sat down to get his bearings. His reverie was broken by the telephone ringing. He reached for the phone.

"Hello."

"This is Brad Ramsey. Welcome to Copenhagen. I'm glad you could come here on short notice. How about meeting for a drink in the hotel bar about 1700 hours? We can talk and then go to dinner. I'll be happy to pick up the dinner tab."

"That sounds like a good plan. I'll meet you in the bar."

McQuesten showered and then stretched out on the bed for a power-nap to get rid of his jet lag. Before dozing off he checked his Beretta pistol to make sure it was in good working order after being out of his control for the eight hour flight. After double-checking the slide action of the pistol, he returned it to his shoulder holster and placed it on the bedside table. McQuesten made no effort to arrange for a wake-up call from the front desk.

The Plaza Hotel bar was a large room with dark wood panels from floor to ceiling. Subdued lighting gave the room a special feeling. The laid back atmosphere made it easy to relax after his flight. McQuesten picked a table in the corner that gave him a wide view of everyone in the bar and both doors. The waitress was a tall blond about thirty years old with her long hair in a French twist. She was cool and sexy in a quiet way. Her manner was different than most American ladies who worked as a hotel bar hostess. She wasn't in any hurry to push drinks and she left him alone. No check-back questions like, "Is everything all right?"

"Jack McQuesten?" said the voice. McQuesten looked up and said, "Brad Ramsey?"

"You got it. Welcome to Denmark," said Ramsey.

"Since you're buying dinner, let me take care of the bar bill," said McQuesten.

"Works for me," said Ramsey.

"Well, let's talk. Tell me what you've learned from the lady informant at the bank," said McQuesten.

"I can tell you this. I've had two meetings with her and she has been very careful about what she says. From what we've been able to put together to date, I'd say we are looking at a potential gold mine. We need to tie up a few loose ends. She isn't holding out on us. The stuff she's given us so far is solid. Our computer geeks and intelligence people have traced the money trail back to Pakistan, however we don't know just yet, where the funds go after her bank passes along the funds through the European Central Bank System wire transfer lines. We're looking closely at a banking operation on the Isle of Man in the Irish Sea. This Irish Sea operation is a reputed money laundering center, but so far, we haven't been able to get the evidence we need to bust them," said Ramsey.

"When do I come into the picture?" McQuesten asked as he sipped his drink and reached for a handful of salted nuts.

"Our lady informant is scheduled to travel to Nice in a few days to pick up new routing numbers that will be used to wire transfer their funds. The clients that we suspect are laundering money refuse to send any numbers through the European e-mail systems. Also, they don't trust first class snail-mail. There are too many potential security breakdowns so everything is done person-to-person, face-to-face," said Ramsey.

"So I travel to France with her and while I baby-sit, try to pick-up on her connections with the criminals. Is that the deal?" asked McQuesten.

"Yes, that's our hope, at least," said Ramsey as he then added, "I've got to get her comfortable with you so then, between the two of you, maybe, we can hit pay dirt."

"Our informant's name is Sophie Goodbody. She's scheduled a vacation day tomorrow from the bank to prepare for her trip to France. I've set up a short trip to the Rosenborg castle for all of us tomorrow. It's always full of tourists and it will be easy to lose anyone from the bank who might be watching her activities. I figure we can take three hours to get acquainted so you won't be strangers when you travel to France. This lady is a history buff and a Danish castle freak. She owns all kinds of books about Danish castles. The time spent at Rosenborg will fit in nicely with her normal routine. You'll just have to pretend that you enjoy looking at Danish castles," said Ramsey.

"Not a problem," said McQuesten.

McQuesten sat in his chair sipping his drink. His mind was rolling over what Ramsey was passing along.

"What are the probabilities that the bank might be suspicious that our lady tipster has passed along valuable secret wire transfer numbers?" asked McQuesten.

"I would say it's almost a zero probability that they suspect anything. Otherwise, why would they be sending her to Cannes to pick up the secret new bank wire code numbers?" said Ramsey.

"Okay, I agree with your assessment on that point. However, I'm still looking for weak spots. I don't see any yet, but it never hurts to ask questions before the operation goes into motion," said McQuesten.

McQuesten and Ramsey finished their drinks and walked outside of the Plaza for a taxi ride to the restaurant.

"We have reservations at one of the most popular spots in Copenhagen. This place is a favorite with the well-heeled tourists and the local "in-crowd." It's called St. Gertrud. We'll go down into the old vaults that were used to store salt, hide wine and munitions back in 1813. The English fleet bombarded St. Gertrud with cannon fire in 1807. During a restoration in 1972 many English cannon balls were discovered. Some of them were returned to the English naval attaché after agreeing not to use them again."

After getting settled into their private little vault dining area, drinks were served with salted snacks. The basement cavern rooms were lit with large candles.

"So tell me about money laundering," said McQuesten as he settled into St.Gertrud's ambiance.

"It's bigger than people would imagine. In Europe it's a major problem because many countries have never agreed on enforcement principles. Some banks are just happy to have business and will route money through their system to get revenues. The ESCB has worked to bring these weak banks into the real world of enforcement but it's hard to accomplish 100% of the time. The criminal elements look for bank managers who are lax on enforcement and run business through those systems."

"What is the penalty if a bank is caught red-handed doing business with crime syndicates and drug cartels?" asked McQuesten.

"For first-timers, it is usually a slap on the wrist that includes a small fine of ten thousand francs. Most Europeans don't concern themselves with money laundering. The ESCB has been forced to set up sting operations to nail some of these unethical schemers. This takes time and it's expensive. This is why our lady source has turned out to be so interesting. We actually have found a concerned bank employee cooperating with us who wants something done about a crooked department head. If we can get some evidence from your trip to France we may actually net some big fish and put them out of business," said Ramsey.

"Okay, now I'm getting a better picture. It would be great if these plans jell and we nail some organized crime operators," said McQuesten.

"Are you getting enough help from headquarters?" asked McQuesten. Ramsey was ready for this question and he rose to the question like he was waiting for it to be asked.

"They sent their files on the Oil for Food Program scandal. Hopefully, something in the files will jump out and help us put together what we have from Goodbody. The files from headquarters shows that the UN received an administrative fee of 2.2% per barrel of oil sold by Iraq, plus another .8% fee per barrel to cover the costs of the UN Iraqi weapons inspection team program. According to headquarters, once the UN gave Saddam the right to sell Iraqi oil to whomever he chose, the door opened up for bribes, kickbacks, graft, smuggling and fraud on a massive scale. Surprisingly, Kofi Annan later approved Saddam's request for the authority to choose all the suppliers of food, drugs and oil machinery equipment."

"I read that too," said McQuesten as he shook his head, and added, "I found it extremely interesting that Saddam ordered the Iraqi Oil Ministry to sell their oil through eight front companies. Basically, it was a simple scam. Saddam sold million of barrels of oil at discount prices, mostly to French and Russians, which they in turn resold into the oil market at world prices. Any company or person who got an oil allocation from Saddam would then kick back money to Saddam in dollars or euros. The year of 2000 was a banner year for Saddam."

"The French and Russian politicians who received special oil allocations from Iraq then defended Hussein and opposed the US and Britain in the UN Security Council after President Bush turned up the pressure against Iraq," said Ramsey.

"I want to study that list of companies and individuals that headquarters sent," said McQuesten.

"Sure, here is a copy of that list I brought along in case you wanted to see the companies involved. It's an eye-opener," said Ramsey.

McQuesten slowly glanced through the list of obscure names of individuals and companies. Liechtenstein Trust – a Swiss registered sub of a Saudi oil company with Taliban connections,; Delta Services – a sub of Delta Oil; a Saudi Arabian oil company; AMEP – African Middle East Petroleum company, ltd, offices in Monaco, approved by the UN to buy Iraqi oil under market prices; Nile & Euphrates company, received three million barrels of oil at $25/bbl; Khalid Gamal Abdul Nasser, Egyptian national who received sixteen million barrels of Iraqi oil at $25/bbl; Munir Abdelnur, AMEP oil executive; Cotecna Inspections, Swiss company hired by Saddam to check imported goods and shipments with ties to Kofi Annan's son; Fakhry Abdelnour AMEP executive; Al Wasel & Babel General Trading; Galp International Trading Corporation; ASAT Trust & Bank Al Taqwa; Youssef Nada & Idris Ahmed Nasreddin –al Qaeda financiers.

Ramsey waited until McQuesten had scanned over the copy of the suspected front companies and then said,

"Naturally, all of the companies and people on this list of benefactors are in a state of denial over their alleged involvement in the OFFP scandal. The former UN head of the OFFP, Benon Sevan, an Armenian Cypriot, has taken an extended leave of absence from the UN to plan his retirement. His current whereabouts are unknown."

"The scam I found most interesting was the "top loading" of oil tankers. A tanker could be loaded with 1.8 million barrels then topped-off with another 272,000 barrels but the bill-of-lading stated the tanker only had 1.8 million barrels," said McQuesten.

"Yes, very tricky. It makes one wonder if we will ever get to the bottom of this OFFP scandal?" said Ramsey.

McQuesten toyed with his drink and let what Ramsey had said sink in his mind and then added,

"It's rumored in Washington that the US Treasury is turning the financial world upside down as they try to track down where Saddam stashed all his ill-gotten money. The Treasury has asked UN members to freeze the assets of Saddam's front companies."

"Between you and me, I think most of the terrorist cells in Europe are thriving. Most Europeans have their minds made up about our war on terror. They have put their heads in the sand and pray the terrorists will just go away," said Ramsey.

*   *   *

Muqtada Abbas sat at his desk looking over the latest balance sheet and income statement of his private Iraqi bank. During the two years Abbas had been the managing director of the bank, its portfolio of Swiss francs and US Treasury notes had grown dramatically. Since the Oil for Food Program began it had become the primary source for hard currency coming into the bank. Because crude oil shipments always settle in dollars, their US Treasury portfolio was now huge. All the bank employees were trained in Baghdad at the Iraqi National Bank. For window dressing, Abbas hired three French women to work on the first floor to handle the coming and going of French banking officials. Only Iraqis were ever allowed above the first floor. No one except Abbas and his trusted number two-man were allowed to see any balance sheet or deposit information.

The Cannes bank of Saddam Hussein actually held only two million in Euros securely stored in the basement vault. All the other funds were deposited at the Bank of France in Paris. These funds were closely monitored daily by Abbas and his second in command, Jassim Salih.

Abbas was a Sunni Iraqi who had grown up in Fallujah, in the heart of the Sunni Triangle. His father and mother were members of the Baathist Party and early supporters of Saddam Hussein. This resulted in his father gaining a lucrative administrative position in the Iraqi oil industry. Abbas attended the best schools and learned to speak English and French. He studied business, international trade and economics in Baghdad and later in London.

Abbas was single so he spent his personal time in Cannes and Juan les-Pins seeking French women. Several attractive lady friends were his favorites but he was careful not to allow his emotions to get carried away by their beauty. It was no secret that the western world, particularly, the USA, was pressuring Iraq about its ties to terrorism. He didn't want any strings of attachment to a woman if he were forced to make a fast career decision. His personal money was deposited in a secret numbered account at a Swiss bank in Zurich. Abbas worked out regularly in the basement of the bank with the six security guards, practicing self defense moves and judo blows designed to disable an opponent. He felt strongly about maintaining a good physical condition. He felt it kept the guards on their toes and would also command respect from them if he was working out with them regularly.

"Do we know when the woman from Denmark is arriving to receive the new routing numbers for our money transfers?" asked Abbas of his number two man, Salih.

"Yes, she will be here in two days. I have all the numbers confirmed, sealed in a traveling packet and ready for her to take back to Copenhagen." Salih was a great detail man and spent time every day re-checking the deposits of the bank before the reports were sent to the Iraqi National Bank in Baghdad.

"Very good," answered Abbas, "I don't want her around the bank too long. In, out, and back to the airport for a plane to Denmark the same day." Abbas had wondered to himself which Badhdad banking official ordered the new transfer codes to be put into place. Perhaps a change was ordered by Saddam himself, who was rumored to be a meticulous detail person.

"Yes, I agree. That would be best," said Salih adding, "All the flight arrival and departure times at the Nice airport are noted on her itinerary file."

Abbas sat at his desk and reviewed his schedule for the day the woman from Copenhagen would arrive. "I want this woman under our surveillance as soon as she gets off the plane. Assign our best security guards to pick her up at the arrival gate and bring her directly here. Where are the pictures of this woman so we know that we're dealing with the correct person?" asked Abbas.

"Yes, I have received several pictures of her taken covertly by our agents in Copenhagen. I don't believe she is aware that we already know what she looks like," said Salih as he handed the pictures of Goodbody to Abbas.

"This is very good work on your part, Salih," said Abbas.

"Praise Allah," said Salih.

One important duty of Salih's many jobs was acting as the custodian for their secret single key crypto code system and the limited distribution of the codes to the authorize users. This crypto system allowed movement of funds to custodian banks such as the Bank of France in Paris. When the Iraqis in Baghdad began the wiring of kick-back funds through their money laundering system, these crypto codes made the flow of funds next to impossible to regulate.

The grounds of the three story Iraqi private bank were surrounded by an eight foot iron fence that was set into granite blocks designed to stop any vehicle attempting to crash the bank building. The streets near the Iraqi bank were filled with three story chic apartments that commanded rental rates considered exorbitant even by most French standards. Every gate into the bank grounds was electronically controlled. Cameras were evident to onlookers from the street. Iraqi security guards, who received their training in Baghdad, patrolled grounds round-the-clock. The six Iraqis assigned to the bank security detail reported directly to Abbas. Two guards were stationed on the first floor during business hours. The other guards worked outside the building and looked after the two black sedans garaged on the premises. Large potted trees and shrubs were growing inside valuable landscaping Iraqi urns placed neatly around the grounds. A small basement room of the bank near the vault served as the physical training room for the guards. All security work details were carefully planned weeks in advance by Abbas. These orders were followed without any question. The guards always dressed in black business suits and carried nine millimeter pistols in shoulder holsters slung under their jackets. They lived together in a small apartment house not far from the bank. Abbas and Salih enjoyed separate apartments in Juan les-Pins.

Ramsey and McQuesten sat in the front seat of their car parked in the visitor lot of the Rosenborg castle. They had a clear view of the bus stop that dropped off castle visitors. Neither had spoken for several minutes, each lost in personal thoughts as to what the events of the day would bring.

"There she is, in the light brown rain coat with a scarf over her head. Just like she said she'd be dressed if she thought no one was following her," said Ramsey, as he added, "Let's go now. We'll move along with the rest of the crowd from the bus. We can separate from them once we get inside the castle."

"So that's Sophie Goodbody. You didn't tell me she was so attractive," said McQuesten.

"I didn't want you to get too excited. Now you know why I like this job. I wish I was going to France with her instead of you. You'll have her all to yourself."

"Yeah, sure," McQuesten said sarcastically.

The two Americans moved along with the crowd and watched Goodbody purchased her tour ticket. The two men purchased their tickets and moved to the back of the crowd. Goodbody picked up on Ramsey and curled an eyebrow as a recognition signal. She looked at McQuesten coolly not yet aware that he was to be her new CIA handler.

"Are you sure this plan of yours is going to work?" ask McQuesten.

"Yes, I paid the castle touring manager five hundred EU's to get the use of a private room this morning. I've known him for some time. His name is Peter Neilson. He has no problem with our meeting alone. Also, he has no clue who we work for or what we're doing. I told him I was part of an American tour group planning a visit here later this year," Ramsey said.

"Okay, I'm in your hands. I hope we can pull this off without any hitches," said McQuesten.

The two Americans and Goodbody moved along with the tour group until they arrived at a narrow passageway which led into another castle chamber. The castle tour manager was standing off to the side and signaled Ramsey.

"All right, it's game time," said Ramsey.

Ramsey signaled to Goodbody and she stayed behind as the other visitors moved through the narrow chamber passageway. The tour manager opened a locked door and ushered them into a small dining room that was set up with table and chairs. "Will this room be satisfactory?" asked the tour manager Neilson. Ramsey nodded yes, and said, "We will need two hours alone here."

"That will be no problem. Here is the key to the door which you may lock from the inside," said the castle tour manager. He moved through the door and left the three alone. Ramsey made sure the door was locked. He then turned to Goodbody.

"Sophie Goodbody, please say hello to Jack McQuesten. He just arrived from Washington, DC and is here to listen to what you have to say about the wire routing codes used by your bank to transfer funds. He is also connected with the US government."

"Nice to make your acquaintance," said Goodbody.

"The pleasure is all mine," said McQuesten.

"All right, let's get started," said Ramsey, as the two strangers looked at each other with personal thoughts going through their minds. McQuesten was trying to hide his thoughts about what it would be like to make love to this beautiful creature.

"We have booked McQuesten on the same flight you are taking to Nice. You will not be traveling as a couple or be seated next to each other. McQuesten will serve as your support back-up if something goes wrong in Nice or Cannes after you have received the new banking codes from the Iraqis. We don't think anything will happen but one never knows in this type of operation. The most important thing is for you to act natural. Let things unfold at their pace. McQuesten will be watching you from a safe distance at all times except when you are in the bank. If something isn't going right you can signal McQuesten by playing with your hair. That will be his signal that you are no longer comfortable and need assistance. Does that seem okay to you, Sophie?"

"Yes, that will be satisfactory," said Goodbody.

Ramsey outlined what the CIA had learned from the secret wire codes Goodbody had delivered to him. "It appears that the Iraqis are using money from the Oil For Food Program to skim cash into the pockets of Hussein and his ruling henchmen. Our contacts in Interpol have told us the private bank in Cannes has assets of twenty billion in stolen funds since Hussein took power in Iraq.

"Quite a little piggy-bank," said McQuesten, and then asked, "But, can we get this money out of his clutches with these new wire transfer numbers?"

"The boys back at headquarters and the Interpol computer hackers in Lyon are highly confident. We have found a paper trail that leads from the Iraqi National Bank to Pakistan, on to Copenhagen plus one more mystery stop before coming to the La Compagnie Fincancises Iraqi Banque, Cannes, France," said Ramsey.

Their meeting continued for another hour. Ramsey then suggested to Goodbody that she travel with them back to her apartment. She had purchased a roundtrip ticket to prove that she had taken a bus back from Rosenborg castle. Goodbody seemed to warm up to McQuesten after they had conversed about the trip to France. The trip back to Copenhagen came off without any problems. Ramsey and McQuesten dropped Goodbody about two blocks from her apartment so she could be seen walking back from the bus stop if she were under surveillance.

*   *   *

After the Paris commuter plane landed at the Nice airport and taxied to the gate, Goodbody deplaned and walked through the concourse. She noticed that the walk eased her apprehensiveness about the upcoming meeting with the Iraqi bank officials. She wondered just where McQuesten might be at the moment. Did he have her in his sight? Was he close-by? She had not seen him since they boarded the commuter flight in Paris.

As she passed the luggage conveyor belt she saw two dark skinned men dressed in black business suits holding a small sign on which her name was printed. She walked up to them.

"I'm Miss Goodbody from Copenhagen."

The men politely smiled, nodded and said,

"Please follow us. We will drive you to the bank."

The ride to Cannes took twenty minutes. Goodbody thought the Iraqis drove cautiously along the highways. Upon their arrival the bank gates swung open, and the car was driven into the garage. Two other men then assisted Goodbody from the sedan. They escorted her into the bank building, up to the second floor and into Abbas' office.

Abbas was sitting at his desk waiting for Goodbody. He did not rise to greet her or smile, but he did ask about her trip in a perfunctory manner. Goodbody was barely finished with her answer when Abbas said,

"Let us get down to our business," and motioned for her to be seated with a wave of his hand.

Goodbody sat down in the chair in front of his desk. She looked directly at Abbas, waiting for him to speak. Abbas appeared stern and began by saying,

"You have been brought here to get the confidential wire transfer codes for our funds that are routed through your bank in Copenhagen. Are you the woman who actually sends out the encrypted wire transfers?"

"Sometimes, I do, but usually three other women do the work," answered Goodbody as she sat on the edge of the uncomfortable chair. At this point, her beauty was not lost on Abbas. He was now sorry he had decided to schedule her to leave the same day. A part of his mind was occupied with day-dreaming and envisioning thoughts about dining with her in a nearby secluded rendezvous and then convincing her to come to his apartment. Something he had done repeatedly with many French women.

Abbas gathered himself and turned on a little charm. He launched into a monologue about how important it was to protect the codes and routing numbers he was about to place in her custody. Goodbody had quickly realized she was dealing with an arrogant Iraqi egocentric. She sat and gazed directly into Abbas' face and tried to appear sincerely interested in his little speech. Finally, after ten minutes, Abbas got up from his chair, walked around the desk and handed her a sealed envelop that contained the codes. She wasn't allowed to see what was in the sealed envelope.

As Goodbody took the envelope from Abbas she sensed that he was still probing at her, trying to find some feminine weakness. She was determined that he wouldn't find any. She compartmentalized all her thoughts about this man and nodded yes to whatever he said. It would speed things along if she agreed with him. She could be on her way back to the airport just that much sooner.

As the guards escorted her out of the bank and back to the sedan for her return trip to the airport, she fought with herself to not look at her wristwatch because she was sure that Abbas was watching from a window. If caught looking at her watch, she felt he'd consider it disrespectful. When she finally was alone in the back seat of the sedan she checked the time. The entire meeting had taken ninety minutes. As the sedan cleared the steel gates to the street, only then did she allow herself to think about her apartment. She had another quick thought of McQuesten, wondering where he was at this moment.

*   *   *

How long have you worked in Paris with Interpol?" asked Sherrie.

"Nine months with the FHT unit and before that, two years in Lyon," answered Marie as she added, "My family is from Juan les-Pins. I enjoy the detective work. My computer classes in Lyon lasted two years and I graduated at the top of my class."

"I know the work we do is challenging. I wish I knew how Interpol obtains all the banking information that we must process. Everyday it seems we're asked to check-out new information from the AMLID," said Sherrie.

"There's something big going in Cannes with the La Compagnie Financiese Iraqi Banque," said Marie as she sipped her cup of coffee.

"Oh yes, I noticed that too. We received inside bank data from an employee at the Vallens Bank in Copenhagen. The American Embassy and CIA passed this along to us. I've been analyzing the data for a week. It is very solid information," said Sherrie as she paused, looked around, lowered her voice to a whisper, and said, "suspected money laundering."

Both women knew they weren't supposed to talk-shop during lunch or coffee breaks. All work was secret and information was disseminated strictly on a need-to-know basis. Gossiping like this could lead to a compromise and retaliation if their work leaked to the wrong people. The Paris branch of Interpol was shrouded in secrecy. No one was supposed to even know of its existence. Both women had been trained in cryptography communications used in computer data communications, most notably electronic funds transfer. Their departments attempted to break-down single key crypto systems that can process several million bits of data per second. The Interpol hackers would create asymmetric, or two key crypto systems signatures, to provide a recipient a means of readily authenticating transmissions for a third party.

That evening Marie visited her widowed uncle Henri in his Paris flat. He had been married to her mother's sister for many years before her death from cancer. Marie visited him regularly to stay in touch with her family. Marie wasn't sure of his age but guessed he was well past eighty. She was never able to learn any details about his early life other than he was married to her mother's sister.

In April of 1945 Uncle Henri was part of a Waffen SS unit that was fighting the Allies in the Ruhr. Back then Uncle Henri was known as Leutnant Heinrich Vossler. His last days in the Waffen SS were spent guarding looted art treasures and gold for Nazi party big-wigs. After the German armies in the Ruhr surrendered, Vossler managed to change his identity. He worked his way to southern France along with thousands of other refugees. He thought it might be possible to hide out in southern France because it had been controlled by Vichy. He had no interest in surrendering to the Allies. Certainly the Russians were to be avoided at all costs. Large numbers of German officers who served in the Wehrmacht, Sicherheitsdienst, and Gestapo disguised themselves as civilians and traveled in trucks and cars with suitcases crammed with gold. By the time he arrived in the Cote d' Azur he had been able to obtain false identity papers and change his appearance with civilian clothes.

Vossler maintained a low profile. He sought any menial work available that would allow him to blend into the war torn society. Being fluent in French made it easier to live his new identify. He worked hard to disguise his German accent. He was most comfortable working on the docks unloading cargo while assisting fleeing Germans book passage on freighters leaving Europe.

It wasn't long before he saw many former Waffen SS officers desperately searching for berths on freighters headed to ports in South America. Argentina was the destination of choice for most of the Waffen SS officers. Through the use of his French language skills Vossler became skilled at arranging passage by bribing French port inspectors to help his German officer comrades to secure passage aboard freighters. For this service he charged all the money he could squeeze from the former SS officers.

As time passed Vossler felt increasingly secure about his personal situation. He left southern France for Paris. He knew he would feel more comfortable in a larger city and there would be better opportunities to meet more women. While establishing himself in Paris he became aligned with the French underworld. He began to do small odd jobs for them. Soon afterward he met a French woman and began courting her, which led to their marriage. He quietly changed his name to Henri Dauphin. Uncle Henri was connected to a waterfront mafia group that had operations in every major French city. He was always interested in stories his niece passed along during her visits. Marie never suspected that her kind elderly uncle had mafia connections.

"So what have you been doing these days, my dear?" asked uncle Henri as he sipped a glass of red wine.

"Oh, the same as always, computer programming simulations, tracking down criminals for Interpol," said Marie. This type of talk didn't cause Marie to have any apprehension because she loved her uncle and he always seemed harmless like many old men who lived alone.

"I know it must be secret, but how do you, as you say, track down the criminals, with a computer?" asked Uncle Henri.

"Well, we receive information from informants, or bank employees who want to help us catch anyone engaged in criminal activity like money laundering," said Marie.

"Do you pay people who work at banks to supply information directly to Interpol?" asked uncle Henri and he honed in on Marie's early statement about where the data comes from for her work to process.

"I'm not sure, but I doubt if Interpol pays any money to people to supply information. Recently we received bank data that confirmed a money laundering ring was operating through Vallens Bank in Copenhagen in conjunction with a bank in Cannes controlled by Saddam Hussein. This data and information was supplied by a dedicated employee who talked with the American Embassy in Denmark. The European Banking Federation (EBF) is keenly interested in this type of inside information. We get tipped-off many times by people who work for banks throughout all of

Europe. I reconstruct the many money transfers and the movement of funds through money centers around all the European banks that disguise illegally obtained proceeds."

"Well, I'm sure it's all very interesting. But this is just too high-tech for an old man like me. Would you like to join me for dinner tonight? There is an Italian restaurant in the next block that serves very good food. I'd be happy to treat if you will join me," said Uncle Henri.

"It sounds delightful. I'd be happy to join you," said Marie.

Later that evening after dinner, he and Marie said their good-byes, uncle Henri sat quietly in his room attempting to remember what Marie had said about her work at Interpol. Finally satisfied that he recalled all the salient points, he checked the phone number of his Paris mafia contact, reached for his telephone and dialed the number. Uncle Henri was justifying his meager existence by giving secret Interpol information to the mafia. He cared little that someone could be in danger of losing their life after he passed along his information. The important thing for Vossler's ego was that he considered himself an active player in the war against the authorities.

The Juan les-Pins Affair

4

Goodbody's office manager at the bank, Gertrude Arnaud, sat at her dining room table studying extra copies of the photographs of Goodbody taken discreetly along the Stroget. These pictures were forwarded to the Iraqi bankers in Cannes. Arnaud enjoyed looking at pictures of beautiful women and these photographs of Goodbody aroused her passions.

While living in Paris, Arnaud worked at several different banks as a back-office wire transfer clerk in the security custody department. One evening she was approached by friends to join their ring of bank employees who generated illegal money for themselves by lending securities from their bank custody vaults to speculators. These back-office clerks covered themselves by placing phony short-term letters of hypothecation in the bank daily tickler files. This activity ultimately led Arnaud into the world of money laundering.

The apartment door bell rang. As Arnaud got up to answer the door she left the photos lying on the table.

"Thank you for coming on such short notice," said Arnaud as she embraced her dinner guest, Maria. Arnaud and Maria had met in a Stroget coffee shop not long after Arnaud had arrived from Paris. The coffee café was a renowned hangout for gay men and lesbians. Arnaud had billed herself as an experienced chef with French cuisine.

"You know that I'm always available for dinner with you," said Maria who glanced at the dining room table setting. Then Maria saw the photos of Goodbody as she stood by the table.

"Who is this gorgeous thing?"

"Oh, that's a woman who works at the bank. She's very nice, and I think, unattached," said Arnaud.

"I see she's sitting with a man. Where was this picture taken, on the Stroget by chance?" Maria asked, as she paused looking at the photo. "Hey, wait a minute. I recognize that guy in the picture. His name is Ramsey, or something like that. I believe he's with the American Embassy here. I think it's possible that he's with the CIA. I've seen him around Copenhagen at private dinner parties. I'm almost positive."

Arnaud's neck muscles cramped with tension. Her facial color became ashen after Maria's comment.

"Are you sure about the man in the picture?

Arnaud pressed Maria since she by now had forgotten about the dinner.

"Yes, I'm real sure. Is there a problem?" Maria asked, "Have I said something that upset you?"

"Oh, it's nothing really, but I've got to make a phone call from my bedroom. Please excuse me," said Arnaud as she felt sick to her stomach. Her mind raced on with private thoughts, "My God, I've sent a courier to Cannes who lunches with a man from the CIA." She knew she was in big trouble. Frantically, Arnaud searched through her list of secret telephone numbers for Muqtada Abbas in Cannes. Finally she found his number and dialed.

"Yes, it's urgent. I must speak with Abbas," Arnaud said to the bank telephone operator. "One moment, please," was all she heard. It seemed to Arnaud that she waited twenty minutes, but Abbas finally came on the line.

"We may have a breach of security. I've just learned the woman courier I sent to pick up the bank codes may be working with the CIA," Arnaud held her breath waiting for a reaction from Abbas.

"How did you come by this information?" Abbas asked calmly.

"Actually, it was by accident. A friend saw a picture of Goodbody lunching with a man. My friend is positive the man in the photo with Goodbody is a CIA agent," said Arnaud.

"And you trust this friend's judgment?" Abbas asked as his voice began to choke.

"Yes, I do," Arnaud answered.

"Do not mention this matter to anyone else until you hear from me," said Abbas as the phone connection went dead.

Arnaud felt a claw ripping in her stomach. Her throat tightened. Sweat was on the back of her neck and rolling down her underarms. She tried to calm herself so she could put up a front to Maria and get through the evening. Her mind raced on almost out of control, if this matter blows up because of Goodbody, Arnaud could see herself being shot some night on a dark street.

Abbas pressed his inter-com button and ordered Salih to come to his office immediately. When Salih walked into Abbas' office he saw that Abbas was upset. Salih announced his presence by saying, "Sir."

"Salih, we may have a complete security bust on our hands. The woman from Copenhagen may be working with the CIA."

"Sir, she has already left the bank. She has the secret codes and is at the Nice airport," said Salih knowing full well that Abbas was aware of these facts.

Abbas looked at Goodbody's itinerary and checked his watch. Her flight was scheduled to leave Nice in thirty minutes. If there was any luck left for him, his security guards could return to the airport, get the woman before her flight departed, and bring her back to the bank for questioning.

"Contact our men on their car phone. Tell them to return to the airport and bring this woman back here to the bank. There can be no foul-up. And tell them to make sure she has the bank code numbers," ordered Abbas.

*　　　　*　　　　*

Goodbody had been standing in line near the security passage-way for sometime. A malfunction with the X-ray machine was causing a big back up in the line of anxious passengers. She happened to glance toward the lobby where she saw two Iraqi bank security guards approaching her with blood in their eyes. She tensed up with fear and became frightened. She reached up with her right hand and began to play with her hair – the signal for McQuesten to come to her rescue. She hadn't seen him in the airport so she could only hope he was nearby. Before she could move the Iraqis were next to her. They pulled her from the security line and began to firmly push her toward the outer lobby doors.

Iron Hand, casually standing about twenty feet away pretending to be reading a paper, saw immediately what was happening and moved to rescue her. He pummeled the first Iraqi with a right hand punch squarely on the jaw. The other man released his hold on Goodbody and swung wildly at Iron Hand with a clinched fist. Iron Hand ducked the blow and grabbed the Iraqi's arm, twisted it backward, then flipped him to the airport floor. He was stunned from hitting the floor and couldn't move.

"Run to the front door. My car is parked outside," Iron Hand yelled to Goodbody.

"Thank God, you showed up. I think they wanted to kill me," said Goodbody as she stepped over the fallen Iraqi.

"Go to the black Porsche convertible," Iron Hand said to her. They scrambled across the car lanes and jumped into the convertible.

Iron Hand got the car started in seconds and the engine roared to life. As he sped away in first gear, the tires squealed from rubber burning as they turned left going up the road ramp on to highway N7. He glanced back at the airport lobby doors and saw neither of the Iraqis. However, Iron Hand didn't notice an Iraqi driver seated in the black sedan parked curb-side, waiting for his two friends.

"What happened at the bank? Why did the Iraqis come back for you?" Iron Hand asked as he pushed the car faster along highway N7.

"I don't know why they came back for me. Everything went well at the bank," said Goodbody as she slumped into her leather car seat.

"Someone has compromised you. Maybe your supervisor at the bank was tipped off by someone." Iron Hand kept a sharp eye on his rear view mirror for the Iraqis. When he came to the junction of E80, he cut over and maneuvered behind some faster traffic.

"We'd better check-in with Ramsey. He may know something about this," said Iron Hand.

"Am I in danger now? I guess my job at the bank is finished," said Goodbody as her precarious situation began to sink into her mind.

"These people play rough. They don't pretend to have any respect for life. The new bank codes may not be useful too long after today if they suspect you're working with the CIA. And yes, I would guess that we are in danger. They probably want to eliminate us."

Goodbody slumped further into the car seat and her face dropped. She fell silent and starred ahead at the traffic. She immediately launched into a personal reassessment of her decision to get involved with the CIA and the American Embassy over her suspicions about money laundering. She started to condemn herself for her actions as her career with the bank now was certainly in jeopardy. Now her life was in danger. "My God, what have I done to myself?" thought Goodbody.

Iron Hand noticed that Goodbody seemed lost in thought, so he continued to talk about their situation.

"It depends on how far up the management line the money laundering ring goes at your bank. My guess is your supervisor won't show up at work if she thinks you've tipped off us. She couldn't pretend to know nothing about the money laundering," said Iron Hand and he added, "Right now, I'm hoping we can get out of here alive. One can never know with whom these people are working. They have enough money to bribe all the police in Cote d' Azur."

Ramsey's telephone buzzed.

"Brad, this is McQuesten in Nice. I'm with Ms. Goodbody. We've got troubles. She picked up the new banking codes but the Iraqis followed her back to the airport and tried to take them. Something has gone wrong. We need your banking gurus to look at these codes before the Iraqis panic and change them again."

"Tell me exactly were you're located," said Ramsey.

"We are traveling west on E80 coming up to a junction with highway N85," answered Iron Hand as he wheeled the car through traffic.

"Okay, take N85 and follow the road signs to Lyon. I'll arrange for an Interpol helicopter pick-up along the road by the Verdon River just past Castellane. One of their men can take your car. You two fly up to Lyon. Call me back when you are aboard the chopper," said Ramsey.

"I like this idea. We'll be watching for the chopper," said Iron Hand as he checked his rear view mirror for the Iraqi bad-guys. The Porsche was doing eighty MPH but Iron Hand kicked it up a few notches and settled into his leather car seat.

*   *   *

Abbas was shaken after hearing the news about Goodbody's escape from his guards at the airport. He felt needle pricks on the back of his neck and a knot was pulling in his gut. After all our precautions, how could this happen? Abbas ordered his men to return to the bank. He dreaded sending word to Baghdad that the new secret bank codes were compromised. Many men in the service of Saddam had been shot for much less. Failure like this wasn't tolerated by Saddam. With whom could the woman have been working as an undercover spy? The CIA? Interpol? Perhaps some Sicilian mafia? Abbas said out loud, "Interpol. It has to be

Interpol in Lyon." He grabbed his cell phone and dialed the mobile car phone number.

"Abdulla speaking," said the Iraqi bank guard.

"What is your location right now?" demanded Abbas.

"Driving west on highway A8 to Cannes," answered Abdulla.

"Turn north at highway N85 and drive toward Lyon. I believe the woman is working with Interpol. They must be headed for Lyon. Overtake them and get back the bank codes!"

"Thank you, sir. We will not fail you again. We are now turning on to N85."

Abbas sat at his desk. He checked the time. How long would it be before he heard from his men, he asked himself. He was sweating, trying to think of all the angles he could play. "Stay cool, stay cool," he repeated to himself. Should he call the police and report that Goodbody had stolen valuables from the bank? He could demand the police set-up a road block on N85. It would slow down traffic and then his men could catch up with Goodbody. Yes, it would work. He reached for his telephone and dialed the Cannes police headquarters. Abbas had given money freely to the Cannes police charities. Now it was time for them to return his favors.

*   *   *

As Iron Hand pushed the Porsche convertible along in heavy traffic he noticed it was backing up. Red tail lights were flashing ahead. An overhead traffic information sign flashed, "Auto Inspection five kilometers ahead. Be prepared for delays."

"Did you notice that message?" Goodbody asked as she turned in her seat to look back in traffic for the Iraqis.

"Yes, if we get tied up in this traffic they'll catch us for sure," Iron Hand said, "There's an exit coming up at Pas de la Faye. I'm going to get off there. Maybe we can drive around the road block traffic inspection."

Iron Hand pulled out his cell phone and dialed Ramsey again. "We've got to leave N85. The police have set up a road block. Is that chopper headed our way, yet?" asked Iron Hand.

"Yes, it's airborne. Give me your exact location so I can relay it to the pilots," said Ramsey.

"There's a road going north to Thorenc. Just before that there is an old castle ruin. We'll be there in twenty minutes," said Iron Hand. "Do you copy this?"

"Yes, I know that area," said Ramsey. "Is it possible for Goodbody to open up the codes and give them to me over this line? I have some ESCB hackers standing by. I believe they may try to move some of the Iraqis' money today before the bank wires go down for the afternoon."

Goodbody heard the question and ripped open the packet she had been given. In a few moments she had the files open. "Yes, I can relay the code numbers," said Goodbody. Iron Hand gave Goodbody the cell phone and watched as she began talking with Ramsey.

"Go ahead. I'll record what you say. I'll play this tape to my Interpol bank computer hackers. I'm sure they will know what to do," said Ramsey.

Iron Hand continued to drive furiously along the winding road. His survival instincts had kicked in as he visualized the Iraqis being not far behind, moving in for the kill. When he wasn't checking his rear view mirror his eyes gazed above looking for the Interpol chopper.

Goodbody continued to talk with Ramsey about the code numbers in the files. There was nothing she didn't understand. She had quickly found the codes and began carefully to pass them to Ramsey. It took about eight minutes to get all the bank data, numbers and authentication codes passed along. Ramsey gave Goodbody a big well-done and signed off. Goodbody exhaled and slumped into her car seat. She looked over at Iron Hand and said,

"I've given him all the codes. Even if they capture and kill us, Interpol should be able to siphon out funds. Abbas won't figure out what happened until it's too late." A warm glow of satisfaction came over her face. She had a good feeling that just maybe she had struck a blow against the terrorists that had murdered her brother.

"I've never trusted bankers. Now I have another reason not to like them," said Iron Hand. Goodbody gave him a look.

"We've got to keep moving. I don't like slowing down on these back roads," grumbled Iron Hand; he added "Where's that Interpol chopper?"

*   *   *

"Salih, you will be in charge of the bank while I'm gone. I can't sit here and wonder what our security guards are doing. I will take a guard to drive the sedan and travel up N85. I have a feeling our men will force the woman back this way. Good-bye for now, but I will be in constant contact with you and our other car. If you learn anything, contact me immediately. Is this all understood?" said Abbas.

"Yes, sir, I will follow all your instructions." said Salih and to himself he whispered, "Praise Allah."

*   *   *

"The Interpol chopper must be lost or they had a breakdown," said Iron Hand. "We're probably going to be on our own until tomorrow. We've got to find a place to spend the night." Goodbody felt a strange feeling running through her body. She glanced at Iron Hand but he didn't notice. The thought of spending the night in a hotel room with him had never occurred to her.

"I think we should find a hotel near the Nice airport. Tomorrow, perhaps Ramsey can arrange for a private jet to pick us up and take us back to Copenhagen. This Abbas guy and his guards will have staked out the airport and hotels in Cannes. He probably has a private spy net work of informants looking out for us too. We should probably get rid of this car and rent one that's not so easy to spot," Iron Hand said thinking out loud.

"There are some good roads to Juan les-Pins on this map. I'll help you get through these small towns," said Goodbody. Iron Hand replied, "Okay, you navigate. I'll drive."

* * *

Abbas sat in the passenger seat plotting his next move. "I must out-think this Goodbody woman and her accomplice," Abbas said to himself. "They may double back and try to hide near the aeroport de Nice Cote d'Azur. Yes, that's what they would attempt to do if they felt we were not thinking clearly. Perhaps a private plane will be waiting for them. Abbas looked at his driver, "Drive toward exit 44 on highway E80. We will park near Super Antibes so we can watch several roads. Look for a black Porsche convertible with two people," said Abbas as he picked up his cell phone and called the other bank sedan. "What is your location?" asked Abbas.

"Sir, we are moving slowly on N85," replied the Iraqi security guard.

"Exit N85 as soon as possible. Come back toward Juan les-Pins on the back roads. I think our prey will be heading back this way. Report back every twenty minutes. Do you understand these orders?" Abbas asked.

"Yes, sir," replied the Iraqi security driver.

* * *

McQuesten and Goodbody went south to Vallauris and finally got through the winding streets to Juan les-Pins. They arrived at the Hotel Ambassadeur, a modern white ten-story hotel that offered underground parking. Registration without luggage didn't cause them a problem in the lobby. McQuesten requested and got the best room available on the second floor. He didn't want to be trapped on an upper floor room that afforded them no easy escape. It was time to again check-in with Ramsey back in Copenhagen. McQuesten dialed Ramsey's private number.

"Ramsey, this is McQuesten. We are now registered at the Hotel Ambassadeur in Juan les-Pins. We need a flight tomorrow from the Nice airport. What can you arrange for us?"

"It shouldn't be a problem. Stay close to the hotel. I'll call back in two hours," replied Ramsey. "Incidentally, just so you'll know, the Interpol chopper stayed around Castellane until it got low on fuel. After that they broke off and headed for their base."

Iron Hand checked his watch: 1630 hours. That would leave time for a shower and then dinner. Room service would be the safest way to get their meals. No need to leave the hotel and maybe be spotted by the Iraqis or some tipster working for them.

"How about ordering some food from room service, Sophie? A bottle of red wine and two steak sandwiches sounds pretty good, doesn't it?" said McQuesten.

"Sounds great. I'm tired and terribly hungry.".

*   *   *

In Baghdad.

"What is going on with the funds transfer unit in Cannes?" demanded Najim Latif, director of the Iraqi National Bank in Baghdad. "No one at this bank has authorized such a large movement of funds."

"There must be a mistake. An unintentional error," replied a bank officer.

"This wire report shows that over twenty billion has been shifted to a bank in Switzerland. Could Saddam himself be moving this huge amount of money and not tell us?" asked Latif.

"Probably that is the answer. I do not wish to ask Saddam about this sizable movement of funds. By doing so, we may cause trouble for ourselves. Perhaps we weren't supposed to know that he was shifting funds to Switzerland," said the bank officer.

"Yes, I'm sure that is the answer. I don't want to bring this matter to anyone's attention. Saddam will know everything in three days when the weekly balance sheet is sent to him," said Latif; as he added, "Very well, we will wait until then. There is no need to pass along information he already knows."

"Yes, I agree that we should say nothing about this to anyone," said the bank officer.

Each man looked into the eyes of the other and saw fear. They knew that if Saddam hadn't authorized this massive shifting of money they were walking dead men. Should they flee the country? This would make them look guilty if something was indeed wrong. Either way they were doomed. They could tell their families to flee to Damascus and then on to Cyprus. Latif returned to his private office, closed the door, and buried his head in his hands. He remembered the pistol in his desk drawer. Should he just end his life now and not wait for Saddam's private security police?

*   *   *

"Sir, this is Salih. One of our informers reported to me that he has seen the black Porsche convertible in Juan les-Pins. It is parked in the garage of the Ambassadeur Hotel."

60

"Excellent work, Salih. Pay your man well for this information," said Abbas as he worked with his cell phone to divert the other sedan and guards to the Ambassadeur Hotel. Abbas could feel a rush of excitement in his body and some tension releasing in his neck. Once his men were in position they would find the woman and her accomplice. He planned to personally put an end to both of them.

"Drive to the Ambassadeur Hotel in Juan les-Pins. When you arrive there go directly into the underground garage," ordered Abbas.

"Praise Allah," said the driver.

*   *   *

Major Falih Zabari sat at his desk in a confined office cramped inside the barracks of the Presidential Guard. He enjoyed smoking one of his favorite thinly rolled Egyptian cigars while checking the watch list and work detail. He was always careful when he had prepared the work detail for the men he commanded. Overhead an old fan moaned to keep the hot dry air and cigar smoke moving. Two windows overlooked a parade ground where his men drilled regularly. A sober portrait of Saddam Hussein hung on the wall behind his desk. Zabari had been chosen by Saddam's executive council to lead two units of soldiers in the Presidential Guard. For this responsibility, he was rewarded with a car and an up-scale apartment in Baghdad, plus an allowance with special price privileges at food and luxury stores that sold western goods. He wasn't above buying certain items in demand and later reselling them to less privileged Iraqis at inflated prices. Corruption was second nature to him.

Zaibari was five feet ten inches tall and carried one hundred eighty five pounds of muscle and toughness. He had a closely cropped haircut and the Iraqi man's mandatory, neatly trimmed mustache'. He regularly worked out with his men to stay in top physical shape by taking part in five mile full-pack marches and hand-to-hand combat drills. He was considered one of the best marksmen with small arms and the AK-47 machine gun. Women considered him handsome by Iraqi standards and he enjoyed the pleasure of their company at his apartment. He was careful not to become emotionally involved with any woman because he knew that there was nothing permanent about his life in the Presidential Guard.

Zabari was a Sunni sect member with strong ties to Saddam Hussein and the Baathist Party. He grew up in an orphanage. After middle school graduation in Mosul he joined a gang of young criminals. He quickly became a gang leader by excelling at ripping off other Iraqis' cars and household luxury items. When he was twenty-three he attended his first terrorist camp in Syria. There he learned about the radical Muslim hatred for the western world and Israel.

A Baathist Party leader approached Zabari and urged him to join the Iraqi army. He was told that in the army he would be able to demonstrate his skills as a leader and make a name for himself. By the time he was twenty-nine he had caught the eye of Saddam's top henchmen. Later he was transferred to the Presidential Guard security forces in Baghdad.

When Hussein wanted enemies eliminated, he called the private security forces to handle the assignment. Zabari never failed to please Hussein when he was ordered to carry out a secret assassination. Soon Zabari was Saddam's favorite hit-man. The killing contracts Zabari handled were completed in style: quickly, quietly and without the evidence of a body that would necessitate some contrived explanation. At the Baghdad headquarters of the Mukhabarat, Saddam's intelligence agency, Zabari was considered invaluable.

The telephone on his desk rang,

"Major Zabari here."

"Major, you have been selected to carry out an important assignment in Cannes, France," said his Army Unit Commander.

"Thank you, Sir. How can I serve the Presidential Guard?" asked Zabari.

"There has been a serious breakdown in discipline at the Iraqi bank in Cannes. The two managers have failed in their responsibilities to protect the assets of Saddam. For this failure, the leadership council has ordered that they be eliminated. There must be no evidence left behind that can be traced to Baghdad. This may be the most important assignment of your career. You must go to your apartment, dress in civilian clothes and then report to the Hussein airport. Then you will be flown by private jet to Nice, France. There you must go to the Iraqi private bank, find the two managers and eliminate them. Do not return to Baghdad until you have completed your assignment. Do you understand your orders, Zabari?"

"Yes, sir," said Zabari.

"Excellent. The pilots of the plane will provide you with your passport, money and the names and pictures of the men you are to eliminate. After you have memorized this information, destroy everything. The pilots will give you instructions how to communicate with them to arrange your return to Baghdad after you have completed your assignment," said his army commander.

"Thank you, sir. I will leave immediately."

"Praise Allah," replied the commander.

The Juan les-Pins Affair

5

Iron Hand stretched out on the king-size bed to relax and fantasized about Goodbody showering. Joining her in the shower seemed like a great idea but she hadn't made any suggestive comments that would have given encouragement. After two days living in the same clothes, he felt scruffy. What was he going to do about it? After ordering their dinner from room service they could only hope it would be decent when it arrived. With Ramsey handling their flight arrangements, Iron Hand wondered when they'd hear about their schedule to leave Juan les-Pins. It wasn't easy being cooped up in a hotel waiting and hoping the Iraqis wouldn't catch up to them. Iron Hand was actually relieved that Ramsey was handling their flight. He closed his eyes to concentrate on his whimsy thoughts of Goodbody naked in the shower. Unfortunately, the fantasy was ruined when his cell phone rang.

"Yes."

"This is Ramsey. I've scheduled a private Lear jet to fly you guys from the Nice airport at 0800 hours and deliver you directly to Copenhagen. Will you be able to hang-in there until then?"

"It shouldn't be a problem. We've had no contact with the Iraqis, but I'm getting some negative vibes that they're working hard to find us," answered Iron Hand trying to sound like a confident CIA officer who never got rattled.

"Okay, here's more good news. There's a US Navy guided missile destroyer anchored in the Nice harbor making a public relations visit. The ship's skipper was a classmate of mine from Annapolis. I've alerted him you may require assistance between now and 0800 hours tomorrow. Copy this cell phone number which will connect you directly to him. His name is Ed Stanley. At the academy we called him, "E-Stan-Boo." When you meet him you'll appreciate the nickname. The destroyer has a chopper aboard which could be used to extract you from a precarious situation, if necessary."

"Great, this sounds great. Thanks for all your good work," said Iron Hand as he signed off. He tucked the destroyer skipper's cell-phone number into his wallet. He'd memorize it later, not now.

The bathroom door opened. Goodbody walked out in bare feet with a large white towel wrapped around her body. Her hair was combed but still wet from a shampoo and she looked refreshed. "Why don't you be a good boy and check on the car and dinner while I fix my hair. Come back in twenty minutes," said Goodbody.

Iron Hand could tell from her voice she wasn't in a playful mood. "Good idea. When I get back here I'll knock this many times," as he held up four fingers. "Don't open the room door for any other reason."

"I understand."

When Iron Hand left the room, he walked toward the elevator but when he passed the stairwell door decided to do a security check. He quietly opened the door to check for any Iraqis hanging out in the stairwell. There were no strangers visibly standing on the stairwell looking for trouble. He listened for several moments and he didn't hear any muffled voices or conversations echoing in the stairwell.

At the elevator, he pushed the down button, waited for the car, but on second thought he decided to walk down the stairs to the lobby, then, go on below to the garage. When he arrived in the lobby, he casually looked around the large atrium and the sunken floor that was used as a dining room for the morning breakfast buffet. Everything seemed normal.

As Iron Hand surveyed the upper floor balconies, he noticed two Arabs standing near the railing about four floors up, engaged in conversation. One appeared somewhat familiar. Perhaps he had been involved in the airport dust-up when he rescued Goodbody. If these Arabs were part of the

Iraqis looking for him, that meant they were already locked-in on this hotel. It probably meant that it would be only a matter of time before they identified their room. The black Porsche was probably the give-away. Some look-out or spy must have spotted them and tipped off the Iraqi bank. Iron Hand picked up a convenient house phone to dial their room where Goodbody was waiting.

"Yes," said Goodbody.

"Sophie, this is McQuesten. I hope you are dressed. I've spotted two Arabs inside the hotel that look familiar. It appears that they may be on to us. We might have to skip dinner and leave right away. They could be stalling for time and then planning to trap us in our room and kill us. I'll be back up there in five minutes. Be ready to leave." Iron Hand put down the telephone and carefully looked around the lobby for any suspicious Iraqis or individuals that appeared to be spying on him.

Iron Hand walked up to the concierge desk and said, "I've developed car problems. I need to rent a car right now. Can you help me?" Iron Hand slipped a one hundred dollar note into the concierge's hand.

"Yes, sir, I'm sure we have something in the garage. There is a newer model green Fiat convertible you can rent. Would that be satisfactory?" said the concierge doing his best to earn the nice tip Iron Hand had given him.

"Yes, I'll take it. Where can I pick it up?"

"I can have it brought to the front door in five minutes. Shall I put the rental charges on your room bill?" asked the concierge.

"Yes, that will be fine." said Iron Hand as he remembered the sick joke about Fiat meaning, Fix It Again Tony.

"Sir, I hope you don't mind my passing along this information, but two Arabs, possibly Iraqis, asked me, not too long ago, if a man and an attractive lady checked into the hotel. They said the lady was tall and blonde."

Iron Hand was surprised at this hearing this news, and then asked, "How long ago did this happen?"

"Thirty minutes ago. Right here at this desk," said the concierge. "I hope you don't mind my mentioning this."

"Not at all, thank you for telling me. But, please, don't talk about this to anyone else. Also, please keep my car rental confidential." At this point he was only interested in averting a dangerous confrontation with the Iraqis. He wondered how long their luck would hold. Iron Hand carefully glanced up toward the fifth floor balcony. The Arab men had disappeared. Another visual check for Iraqis in the lobby proved negative.

Iron Hand walked to the elevator and passed through the open doors. He pressed the second floor button but also decided to press several upper floor buttons to confuse any Iraqis if they were watching. He carefully worked his way back to his room and knocked four times. Goodbody came to the door and asked, "Who is it?" "It's me, McQuesten, Open up." As Goodbody opened the door Iron Hand heard the near-by elevator doors opening. He glanced back and was relieved when he saw the room service waiter bringing their food.

"Over here, garcon," Iron Hand took the food cart and tipped the waiter twenty Euros. The waiter left with a smile. As Iron Hand hurried the cart into the room, Goodbody grabbed a steak sandwich and began devouring it; Iron Hand opened the bottle of red wine and poured two glasses. Time didn't allow them to enjoy the meal but it was important to get some nourishment. Neither of them spoke while they consumed their meal.

*   *   *

Abbas had tipped a hotel bell hop fifty Euros to get the room number of Goodbody and McQuesten. He then sent his men to the garage with orders to disabled the Porsche. After completing this, they would then focus on eliminating the Danish woman and her accomplice.

As Iron Hand swallowed his red wine, he decided to look through the security peep-hole in the door. He saw two men who appeared to be Iraqis milling around in the hall. Without alarming Goodbody, he walked to the sliding glass doors on the balcony and surveyed the grounds below the second floor. There was no one in sight. Iron Hand slowly opened the glass door and looked along the side of the hotel. There were no Iraqis visible. After waiting so long for room service, McQuesten had the beginnings of a headache. He hoped the food would drive the pain away.

"Sophie, take a look through the peep-hole in the door. Tell me if you recognize any of the men in the hall," said Iron Hand, as he checked his Beretta pistol safety switch and made sure he would be ready for any action.

Goodbody looked through the peep-hole, turned back to Iron Hand and said, "I don't recognize them"

"With those guys walking the hallway, we may have to leave this room via the balcony," said Iron Hand.

Goodbody looked apprehensive. Iron Hand quickly added, "This room has a fire escape ladder inside the flower box. We will use it to get to the ground below our room. Do you think you'll be able to climb down this rope ladder?" asked Iron Hand.

"I'm game," said Goodbody; she paused and added, "And another thing, don't ever leave me alone as long as we are running from these Iraqis."

"I like the idea of not leaving you alone," Iron Hand said with a smile and sparkle in his eyes.

They hastily finished their lunch. Iron Hand pointed to the window and led the way to the rope ladder. It was possible, thought McQuesten, that the Iraqis had been in the room next door, listening to their conversations through the walls.

Iron Hand carefully looked out the sliding glass door before dropping the rope ladder from the flower box container. He double checked the security of the ladder so they would not collapse the ladder with their weight. Goodbody was still looking apprehensive so Iron Hand said,

"I'm going down first, so if there's a problem I can help you get to the ground."

"I like the sound of that."

Iron Hand checked his pistol in his pocket and satisfied himself that he was ready to climb down the rope ladder. He glanced at Goodbody and she smiled back. He climbed over the railing and lowered himself directly down the rope ladder without any trouble. He looked back at Goodbody and waved for her to start down. She athletically climbed the railing and brought herself down to the ground.

After they were safely on the ground, Iron Hand took Goodbody's hand and they walked toward the garage. His plan was to walk up from a garage stairwell to the front entrance and pick up the green Fiat. As they walked through the garage, Goodbody caught her breath, pulled back and said, "Those two men ahead of us are the Iraqis who grabbed me at the airport."

"Yeah, I recognize them too," said Iron Hand.

Each Iraqi had pulled his pistol. They moved toward Iron Hand and Goodbody. The first Iraqi fired his pistol but the shot went wild. Iron Hand grabbed Goodbody and ducked down between two parked cars. A second shot from the Iraqis missed Iron Hand and hit the cement support pillar. One Iraqi kept moving forward toward them with his pistol pointed ready to fire.

Iron Hand pulled out his Beretta, aimed at the charging Iraqi and squeezed off one shot. He heard a moan from the man and saw the Iraqi slump to the garage floor. The other Iraqi then moved around behind a car and began to creep slowly toward Goodbody and Iron Hand.

Goodbody froze on the garage floor as Iron Hand rolled out into the driveway to get a better view of the Iraqi. Iron Hand looked under the parked cars to see if he could follow what the Iraqi was doing. Iron Hand heard one shot from the Iraqi and the bullet bounced off the floor. Iron Hand fired his pistol twice as the Iraqi came bolting around a parked car. The bullets from Iron Hand's Beretta found their mark. Iron Hand slowly walked over to check the men and found they were dead. He reached down and picked up a nine millimeter pistol lying on the cement floor next to one of the dead Iraqis. He tucked it into his belt. He then dragged the bodies of the dead men between two cars. Satisfied that he had cleaned up the messy results of their shoot-out as best he could, he called to Goodbody.

"It's okay now, Sophie. We have got to get out of here. Let's go up those stairs to the front door. I have a car waiting for us." Goodbody looked at the two motionless men on the garage floor and shuddered slightly. She grabbed at Iron Hand's arm, moved closer to him and locked her arm around his. They arrived at the front entrance and found the concierge was standing by the Fiat.

"We heard some noise, like a car back-firing. Is everything all right?" asked the concierge.

"Yes, everything is just fine," said Iron Hand as Sophie got into the passenger seat. Iron Hand started the car. It sounded good. As they began to pull away from the entrance and drive down the driveway, Iron Hand looked at Goodbody and said, "Sophie, duck down in your seat. If any of these Iraqis are watching this car maybe they won't see you." Iron Hand checked his watch as he wheeled the Fiat into the street. It was 1900 hours. Where could they go hide until tomorrow morning? Fortunately, the traffic was not congested and the car responded well to McQuesten's heavy foot on the accelerator. After a few moments, Goodbody was sitting upright and seemed to enjoy the wind blowing through her hair. It was good to be out of the hotel room moving away from the Iraqis. Iron Hand's mind began to sort out the possibilities of a different hotel to hole-up for the evening.

*   *   *

The old Frenchman, Claude Seurat peered from an upstairs window of his building in downtown Juan les-Pins. He always checked the streets below his windows to see if any policemen were staked-out around his business. He used two rooms on the second floor as his gambling book clearing office. He counted his cash and saved betting slips in old shoe boxes just long enough to ensure that his clients who won a bet were paid. He didn't believe in keeping the old betting slips a long time. It was too dangerous to save betting slips that could fall into the hands of the police prosecutors if they ever raided his building. The windows were shaded by old Venetian blinds that purposely hadn't been cleaned for years. It was next to impossible for someone to peer through the dirty windows and see the gambling business. Seurat had twenty-five men on his payroll serving as runners for his gambling business. They were connected by the best cell phones he could buy. He could easily arrange a conference call with his runners by pressing several numbers and a call letter code button. By most criteria, Seurat ran a small time gambling operation but he made a good living by controlling his costs and personally handling the day-to-day management.

Abdul and Ghazi, who worked as guards at the Iraqi bank in Cannes, were regulars at Seurat's restaurant. While off duty, the two Iraqis quickly became favorites of the restaurant staff because they were generous tippers. They were constantly looking for beautiful French women. The two Iraqis spent money freely buying drinks for women and gambling on horses, soccer games and lotteries. When they learned about Seurat's network of runners they asked Seurat to have his men act as additional surveillance for the bank. If Seurat's runners passed along any information that was of interest to the Iraqis they would be rewarded with cash. Abdul had just telephoned Seurat to alert his runners to look out for a man and woman driving a green Fiat convertible through the streets of Juan les-Pins. There was a good reward promised for the runner who brought accurate information of the location of the Fiat and passengers. Seurat liked this kind of side action. It gave his men an opportunity to make extra money while keeping them on their toes. It also guaranteed that the two Iraqi guards would continue to be regular customers of his restaurant.

The Juan les-Pins Affair

6

Iron Hand and Goodbody sped through the narrow winding streets of Juan les-Pins but not quite fast enough to draw attention from the local gendarme. As Iron Hand drove the Fiat with determination, he remembered a small hotel near the water's edge which would be a perfect hide-away for the night. He'd been through enough excitement for one day. A good rest was what he needed before their rendezvous with the plane at 0800 hours tomorrow. As Iron Hand maneuvered the car to the hotel, Goodbody glanced slyly wondering what the evening with McQuesten might bring. McQuesten had some interesting qualities but was he the kind of man she could become serious about? This question had nagged in her mind since their first meeting.

Iron Hand eased up on the gas pedal. "I know you don't want to be left alone again, but around the next corner there's a small hotel near the waters edge. It's called Hotel La Villa Juanaise. When I turn at the corner, I'll slow down to let you jump out of the car. Go into the hotel and rent a room. I'll take the car away from here and leave it.

I have a feeling that the Iraqis know this car. After I get it parked, I'll take a cab back to the hotel. The whole caper will take about fifteen minutes."

Goodbody looked at him with doubt in her face but reluctantly agreed, "All right, but please make sure it's just fifteen minutes."

"Tell the manager you are expecting me so he'll give me the room number."

Iron Hand arrived at the corner and slowed down to let Goodbody jump out of the car. He eased off the gas and gently touched the brakes. Goodbody athletically hopped from the car and moved quickly to the sidewalk. She turned her head and watched as Iron Hand drove down the street. She wondered if she would see him again.

As soon as Goodbody was clear of the car, Iron Hand pressed down on the accelerator and the convertible sprang to life. He had gained a sixth sense that warned him if someone was following him. Perhaps this sixth sense in his mind was what had kept him alive all these years. This special sense was beginning to kick-in its vibes, but Iron Hand wasn't paying attention.

Several blocks later, as he pulled up for a red light, a black sedan drove up behind him. Being preoccupied with Goodbody and the hotel, Iron Hand had foolishly left no room to maneuver the Fiat away from the other car directly in front of him. He was boxed in the traffic lane. Two burly Iraqis got out of the black sedan and ran up to the car with guns drawn. They motioned for Iron Hand to get out. They then pushed him back toward their sedan. Another Iraqi jumped into the convertible, drove it to a nearby parking lot and left it there with the keys in the ignition. Unluckily for Iron Hand, the sidewalk was deserted when the Iraqis approached him while he sat helplessly in the convertible.

After forcing Iron Hand into the sedan at gun point, they took him for a wild fast ride through the streets back to Cannes. Iron Hand soon found himself in a smelly basement room of the Iraqi bank building filled with physical training equipment and weight lifting stations. The room was about fifteen by twenty with only one door which was locked. The room had no windows from which he could attempt an escape. There was nothing to do but wait until his captors decided to what they wanted to do with him. Every personal item was taken from his pockets along with his Beretta pistol. Presumably, they were examining his stuff to figure out his real identity and why he was protecting Goodbody. Iron Hand guessed it was approximately 2200 hours but there was no way to be sure. He found a chair and dozed off. The noise of keys rattling in the door lock awakened him from his nap.

He jumped up and prepared himself for whatever was going to happen.

"My name is Muqtada Abbas. I am the managing director of the Iraqi private bank here in Cannes. What have you done with this woman?" asked Abbas as showed a photograph of Goodbody to Iron Hand.

"My name is Jack McQuesten. I'm not sure where she is at this time. She wanted me to protect her from your men. That's all I can say."

"It does you no good to tell me lies," said Abbas as he continued to probe McQuesten. "Who are you working for; Interpol, the CIA or a European crime syndicate? We want the truth now, or we will resort to unpleasant methods to make you talk."

"Forcing me to talk won't do you any good. There are plenty of men like me who will take my place. The smartest thing you could do for yourself would be to leave this bank and go to Switzerland with your money. Very soon, now, Saddam will be through ruling Iraq. The western allies will topple his regime and all of you will be in the street or hiding from the police," said McQuesten bravely.

"You are like the typical American dog, full of empty promises and superior attitudes about how to rule the world from Wall Street and Washington, DC," said Abbas as he signaled his two men with the wave of his hand to leave the room. The guards left the room but kept the door ajar so as to return without wasting time putting a key into the lock.

"Abbas, there is no way you can get your bank codes back. The numbers have already been given to Interpol bank analysts and they are undoubtedly switching your money into a safe account controlled by the ESCB authorities. You're toast as soon as Baghdad figures out you've allowed the new codes to be stolen. You've screwed up big-time."

McQuesten attempted to stand his ground even though he knew his situation was precarious. When you have no hand to play the only thing to do is bluff.

"You lie, you American dog. You'd say anything to save your skin. I promise you, you'll never leave here alive," said Abbas as he started to move toward McQuesten.

Iron Hand dropped into a protective position as the two men circled each other, looking for an opening to strike the first killing blow. Abbas faked a lunge and spun on his left foot and kicked hard at Iron Hand. The blow caught Iron Hand in the side and knocked him down. Abbas was on top of Iron Hard and tried for a neck choke hold to cut off any air going to Iron Hand's lungs.

Iron Hand followed up with an elbow into Abbas' mid-section and a twisting arm and fist move to his head. Abbas released his choke hold and fell back. Iron Hand straightened up and let Abbas get to his feet. Abbas steadied himself and rose up to do one of his spin moves with a leg blow at Iron Hand. This time Abbas dropped to the floor and swung his left leg at Iron Hand to knock him down. Iron Hand jumped up and Abbas's leg went under him, missing completely. Iron Hand jumped down on top of Abbas and had him in a full Nelson hold, pressing him into the floor mat. "Have you had enough of this?" asked McQuesten. The next thing McQuesten remembered was the blow to his head by some unseen hand. Obviously, Abbas's men had been sneaking a look at their boss; realizing that he was in trouble, they came to his rescue.

Abbas sat at his desk analyzing his options now that he was reasonably sure the new banking codes were not going to be retrieved. He had determined it was true that someone within the ESCB system had transferred billions of dollars from the balance sheet of the bank. If it had happened as the American dog had said, then it was now just a matter of time before Saddam's death squads arrived for his skin. Abbas knew he was in trouble but he was smart enough not to panic. He didn't want to make his situation worse than it already was.

Although Salih was not directly involved with the American in the basement training room, he did learn that something huge had happened with the bank's funds within the ESCB system. One of his buddies in Baghdad had telephoned and alerted him it looked like they were in trouble because so much money had been moved from the balance sheet. Nothing definite was said by his Baghdad friend, but the message was that it didn't look good for him and Abbas. Saddam's henchmen at the National Bank of Baghdad were talking about the movement of money to an unfamiliar bank in Switzerland.

Salih sat behind his desk for several minutes attempting to estimate the gravity of his personal situation, now that Baghdad was aware that funds of the bank had been siphoned away by law enforcement hackers. Salih remembered his father's words of wisdom, passed along to him when he was a young man growing up. His father had taught him to recognize when his situation was untenable. In cards and life one must know when to throw in the hand you have been dealt. His father told him to never back a lame horse and never try to bluff if you are holding a weak hand.

Salih wondered how a law enforcement agency, perhaps Interpol, had been able to break through the bank security so easily. Salih imagined what his friends back in Baghdad were now saying about him. They could have an office pool organized to bet how long he and Abbas would live. Salih had lived in France long enough to know he didn't want to return to Iraq under suspicion and face a firing squad. He plotted his strategy for survival. He knew that he needed cash to facilitate an escape. He could feel the pressure building in his head, and the tightening of his neck muscles. His mind reeled with ideas about his potential for survival. He decided to pay a visit to the basement physical training room to get a look at the prisoner.

Salih walked down the back stairs that led to the basement training room. He approached the door to the training room and looked through the peep-hole to see Iron Hand in a chair with his hands tied. Salih thought the prisoner looked like he had been hit by a freight train.

Salih motioned to the security guard, "Open the door and stand guard just by the door." As the guard opened up the door, Iron Hand looked up and mentally got himself ready to receive more abuse. As he looked at Salih he thought, "Who's this little guy, a new sick tormentor?" There was nothing Iron Hand could do but sit in his chair and take what ever punishment this little man was going to give him.

Salih came close to Iron Hand and whispered, "You'll never get out of here alive unless I help you escape. Do you understand what I'm saying to you?"

"Why would you help me?" replied Iron Hand as he suddenly saw a ray of hope out of his predicament.

"Because this bank is probably finished; it's only a matter of time before Saddam's death squad will show up to make us all pay with our lives for our stupidity. They will take us back to Iraq and kill us in a dirty prison cell," said Salih, as he waited for a reaction from Iron Hand. "It's simple, I help you get out alive and you provide me with enough money and safe passage out of France to South America. Fifty thousand dollars should do the trick. If you agree, I will help you. It will not be easy for me to get you out of here past all the guards, but it's the only chance you have getting out alive. I know how these people work. They will kill anyone on Abbas's orders. Think about the deal that I'm offering you."

Iron Hand had read about this type of sick trick used in the Orient by Chinese warlords. Make a prisoner think he is going to be rescued to get up his hopes, but then tell him later the deal has fallen through - a perverted trick, used by sadistic interrogators to crush the will of a prisoner to resist further.

Unknown to Iron Hand was Salih's Shiite affiliation. Salih had grown up in Najaf and had become tired of Abbas and his Sunni elitist superior attitude. If Abbas was so smart, why were they in danger of being killed by a Baghdad death squad? Undoubtedly Saddam had ordered his assassination squad to Cannes. If this were true, his life could be measured in hours, not days. Salih committed himself to his plan because it was the only way to stay alive. This American prisoner would be his passport ticket out of France. He was obviously connected with a large police security force capable of funding his escape to South America. Salih continued to look at Iron Hand's tired face and disheveled appearance.

"I will return in ten minutes with one of the French women from the first floor. She has been my mistress, but the guard outside this door has recently also had his eyes on her. She will distract him for a few moments by flirting. I will overpower him and then he will be left here in this room. You will dress in his clothes and walk with me and my mistress out to a car. We will then use the sedan to leave the bank compound. Think about this offer I am making to you. Or, you can remain here and be beaten senseless by the security guards until you tell them what they want to hear.

Iron Hand nodded his head in agreement. He whispered, "I'm sure we can get the fifty thousand dollars that you require."

"Excellent. I will return shortly," said Salih.

Salih walked to the door and knocked once. The guard opened the door and looked in at Iron Hand and then motioned to Salih to come out of the room. Salih looked at the guard and said,

"I will return shortly. I will bring a woman with me to soften up the prisoner."

"Very good, sir," said the security guard.

Salih returned to his desk on the second floor of the bank by running up the back stairwell. He wanted to get a sense of where the other guards were stationed and what Abbas was doing in his office. As he walked by Abbas's office, he noticed the personal items of Iron Hand lying on the desk outside of Abbas's office. Salih scooped up the entire pile of belongings and carried them into his office. He put them into a black briefcase he normally used while running errands in Cannes.

At this point he called his mistress, Etta, and told her to meet him near the stairs on the first floor. Salih now had his plan in motion. Etta would do anything he asked of her. As she smiled to him in the stairwell, Salih told her to flirt with the security guard in the basement. They would then take a ride in the sedan and have a wonderful evening together that she would never forget. Etta said nothing, but she nodded her approval his plan. As they walked down the stairs to the basement training room Salih passed the small briefcase to Etta and told her to hang on to it until he asked for it back.

Salih approached the security guard and said, "Open up the door and let me go in for a moment. I need to get the prisoner ready for this woman."

The guard did as he was told and then turned his attention to the French lady who had been the object of his affection for sometime. Etta immediately began flirting to get the complete attention of the guard.

Salih entered the basement training room, looked at McQuesten and motioned him to remain quiet. Salih picked up a small two-pound weight used for exercising and walked back to the open door. He walked up behind the guard, who only had eyes for the French woman, and struck a quick blow behind his ear with his fist and the two-pound weight. The guard slumped to the floor unconscious. Salih picked up the guard by his arms and dragged him into the basement room. He then untied the cords that held McQuesten to the chair. Salih straightened up. He looked at McQuesten,

"Get the guard out of his clothes and put them on. Do it quickly." He reached for the tape he had in his pocket and taped the guard's mouth. He then taped the guard's ankles and wrists behind his back after McQuesten had removed the guard's clothes.

McQuesten was not in any position to question Salih about what was going to happen next. He followed orders and was glad to be getting out of the basement cell. He wondered if this was some kind of ruse or elaborate trick to move him from the bank building so they could kill him in a dark alley. He cautioned himself to keep up his guard and be prepared for tricks. His hopeless predicament was, however, improving.

They reached the first floor and headed for the garage where the sedans were always ready. Salih pushed a button in the garage that opened the driveway gates. There was no guard inside the garage to question Salih. Suddenly, a security guard appeared from the grounds and started moving toward McQuesten who was dressed in a suit that obviously didn't fit. The guard walked around McQuesten and up to Salih. He started to reach for his gun. McQuesten moved next to the guard and with one blow to the chin knocked him out. The man slumped to the garage floor. McQuesten dragged his body off to the side of the garage and then jumped into the back seat of the sedan. Salih and Etta climbed into the front seat and nonchalantly acted like business as usual, going into town on an errand. The keys were in the ignition and Salih guided the sedan out of the bank compound and into traffic, he turned to look at Iron Hand, saying,

"All right, where do we go from here, Yank?"

"We've got to distance ourselves from this bank building. I don't care where we go, but please do it fast!" said McQuesten.

"Etta, please give the briefcase to the American," said Salih as he pushed the sedan into a faster lane.

McQuesten looked strangely at Etta as she smiled passing over the briefcase. McQuesten took it from Etta, opened it and saw his Beretta, cell phone and other personal items.

"Do you trust me now, Yank?" asked Salih.

"Yes, and it's a good thing," said McQuesten as he picked up his Beretta pistol and checked the action and ammunition. It felt good in his hand and he thought to himself, "Come to Papa." The escape had happened so quickly, Iron Hand was still dazed by all the action. He had cobwebs in his head from the blows he had taken from the Iraqis. He began to breathe deeply to get some oxygen into his blood. He thought this might bring him around faster.

*   *   *

Etta Ravier grew up in Paris with two older sisters in an apartment off Victor Hugo Circle. Their father was a plant manager of a glass manufacturing company that had joint venture contracts with high profile American glass corporations. Their mother remained home and managed the family affairs.

Etta graduated from a private school for girls, passed her entrance examinations for university, and completed two years before leaving school to "get on with her life" as she often told her mother and father. Etta craved the excitement of Nice and Cannes and not a marriage that her mother was attempting to arrange with a young French banker.

Soon after Etta arrived in Nice, she attended a party in Juan les-Pins with a new friend. There she learned about a job opening at La Compagnie Financiere Iraqi Banque, Cannes. She arranged for an interview and was hired immediately after Salih saw her athletic body, flashing eyes and well formed breasts. It wasn't long afterwards that Salih was flirting regularly with Etta on the first floor of the bank. The other women, married with families, were amused at the attention Etta received from Salih, the man who was second in command at the Iraqi bank.

The Juan les-Pins Affair

7

As the Lear jet descended into the Nice airspace, Ramsey moved up into the cockpit jump seat behind the pilots and buckled up to ride the last hundred miles.

"What is our ETA?" asked Ramsey.

"Looks like twenty one minutes. The air controllers have given us landing instructions and clearance. No other incoming traffic within one hundred miles," said the pilot.

Ramsey had flown into Nice before. He easily remembered the beauty of the Cote d' Azur Mediterranean scenery of the 17th & 18th century buildings. The amenities of hotels, swimming pools, gardens and fountain squares disappeared from his mind however, when thoughts of McQuesten and Goodbody returned. He hadn't heard a word from him since their last conversation. He should have had confirmation of their rendezvous. No communications could mean a high probability that there was trouble.

*   *   *

Goodbody remained in her room since she had checked into La Villa Juanaise Hotel at 1900 hours. She had ordered a late dinner and now breakfast from room service. She was savvy enough to not to leave her room and walk around the hotel, restaurant or the sandy beach. This could expose her to a chance sighting by a spy for the Iraqi bank. There was nothing she could do but wait until McQuesten made contact. If worse came to worse, she would contact the American Embassy in Copenhagen. Obviously, McQuesten must have been the victim of foul play. She could only hope that he was still alive. Sitting in her room watching TV, she thought, that at least there wasn't any news being reported about a dead American found in the streets.

*   *   *

Salih and Etta drove into the hills over Juan les-Pins until they found an inconspicuous place to park. After parking the car, Salih and Etta leaned back and began talking to Iron Hand in an effort to get him oriented and rational. Iron Hand slowly began to come around from the blows to his body and head he endured from the malicious security guards. Now it was time to get some nourishment.

"I need to eat," groaned Iron Hand in a weak voice while resting his head in his large hands.

The threesome drove on again until they found a small bistro whose menu featured la petit dejeuner. After getting Iron Hand out of the back seat and into the bistro, Etta looked at Iron Hand and said,

"I will be happy to order your food. Just tell me what you want." Etta was beginning to feel sorry for this big American whom she hardly knew.

"Good idea. I'd like scrambled eggs, toast and coffee," said Iron Hand in a groggy voice.

The French waiter looked down his nose at the three of them in a typical condescending manner. The waiter was impatient with everything once he figured out that there was an American seated at his table.

Etta looked up at the waiter and said,

"Je desire du pain avec du beurre et du fromage, et ensuite une omelette. Café, s'il vous plait."

Upon hearing the food order spoken in French, the waiter reacted like he was dealing with a person worthy of his attention. He returned to the kitchen. Shortly thereafter, the black coffee appeared. Iron Hand drank his cup of coffee quickly and signaled for a refill. The waiter appeared annoyed and tried to ignore the request. Etta got the waiter's attention,

"Encore du café, s'il vous plait."

The bistro walls were decorated in old French prints, La Marque du Temps qui Passe, by Michel Pernes and some old Masters, plus many black and white photographs from WW II. The tables were all covered with white cotton cloths and old silverware that had been used for years. It was clean and the smell of food from the kitchen made everyone hungry. It appeared that they were the first customers of the day.

As the cobwebs in Iron Hand's head receded, the little gray cells in his brain told him that Salih was becoming nervous about when he would get his fifty thousand bucks. Obviously, Salih was in no mood to hang around Juan les-Pins.

Iron Hand pulled out his cell phone and began to punch out Ramsey's number as best he could. He paused for a moment and said,

"I've got to communicate with some of my people. You don't suppose that Abbas put a bug on this cell phone, do you?"

"No, Abbas is smart, but he's no electronic genius," said Salih as he stifled a small laugh at the question about Abbas planting a bug in McQuesten's cell phone.

Iron Hand accepted Salih's comment and continued to dial the number on his cell phone. Iron Hand got up from the table and walked to the other side of the room. For a few moments there was nothing and then Ramsey's voice came on the line.

"Hello, who's calling, please?"

"Ramsey, is that you? This is McQuesten here. Where are you?"

"McQuesten? Where have you been? I'm at the Nice airport with the Lear jet. Is everything all right? Fill me in. I was becoming concerned."

"Listen, Brad, I'm lucky to be alive. I'm with two people who helped me escape from the Iraqi bad-guys. I owe this guy Salih fifty thousand bucks for engineering my escape. We can talk about that later. Right now I'm concerned about Goodbody. I haven't seen her for about ten hours. In case someone is monitoring this call, I won't tell you where I left her last night. I'll go to her location, pick her up and then meet you at the airport. I should be there in one hour if all goes well. I'll be in contact again shortly. You have my cell phone number if you need to contact me. Talk to you later," said Iron Hand.

McQuesten looked at Salih and Etta. They were lost in conversation as they finished their café. Salih seemed to be relieved that he wasn't going back to the Iraqi bank and face certain death at the hands of one of Saddam's goons. Aside from that, everyone appeared better after finishing their meal. Since the bistro was empty of other patrons McQuesten felt a little more relaxed. He walked back to the table and said,

"Okay, here's what we must do. We have to go back to a hotel near the beach and pick up Goodbody. Hopefully, she is there still waiting for me. After we find her, we can go to the Nice airport. There is a plane waiting there for me. I will make arrangements for you to be paid your money for aiding my escape. Does this sound like a plan you are comfortable with?"

The owner of the bistro was sitting in the corner at a table that looked like his private preserve. He studied the American carefully, trying to make some connection. McQuesten was oblivious to the little Frenchman. Salih was too busy studying Etta to notice the old man.

"Yes, it sounds like a good plan. I'll drive the car, if you don't mind, since I'm used to this car and these streets. You can ride in the back. Etta will ride up front with me," said Salih.

"That's fine. Let's get going," said McQuesten; he felt better after his meal. If they could find Goodbody and get to the airport this whole caper could be all wrapped up, thought McQuesten. He piled in the back seat and tried to enjoy his ride through the resort town. Maybe things were going to get better for the good-guys,thought McQuesten.

At this time in the morning there was little traffic in Juan les-Pins. McQuesten easily directed Salih to the hotel on Rue Saint Marguerite where, hopefully, Goodbody was still ensconced. Salih slowed down in front of the hotel and looked back at McQuesten. Iron Hand was in a combative mood and said,

"Let me out here and you park in front by the curb. I will go in and bring her out. Don't get nervous if I'm not back in five minutes. This may take a little extra time," said McQuesten in the tone of voice used by a commander.

Salih looked at Iron Hand and nodded his approval. Etta smiled and went along with the program. She was thinking that this was the most exciting thing that had ever happened to her in her life. She didn't know that people actually lived like this.

McQuesten walked up to the hotel clerk behind the registration desk and said, "What is Ms. Goodbody's room number? She is expecting me even though I'm a little late."

The room clerk looked over McQuesten curiously trying to place him with Ms. Goodbody. He thought that everything seemed on the up and up but still he wasn't sure.

He turned away from McQuesten, picked up a telephone, and called Goodbody's room. She must have said the right things because he quickly hung up the telephone and said, "She is in room twenty-one. She asked for you to come right up."

McQuesten took the stairs two at a time and located the door of room twenty-one. He knocked four times, which was his old signal that everything was A-okay.

"Where have you been?" said Goodbody but then she threw her arms around him and gave him a kiss on the mouth; a kiss that she knew he wouldn't soon forget. She continued to hold him close as he spoke to her.

"It's been a long night. I'm lucky to be alive. Is everything all right with you?"

"Yes, I'm fine, but I worried myself almost to death. What happened, Jack? Where have you been?" she repeated.

McQuesten thought it was nice to hear her say his first name. Finally, she relaxed her arms and stepped back from him.

"We don't have time to go into everything. But I will tell you later. I've got two people waiting outside the hotel and we're going to the airport. Ramsey is there with the plane to take us to Copenhagen. The Iraqi private bank in Cannes is probably out of business. I'm not sure, but I think Ramsey will have more information about what happened at the bank." said McQuesten.

"Good for our side," said Goodbody as she grabbed her purse. As she went out the door, McQuesten noticed the handle of a nine millimeter pistol protruding from her purse. It had slipped his mind that he had given her the gun in the garage at the Ambassadeur Hotel. McQuesten now thought that just maybe Goodbody wasn't a typical beautiful-but-helpless female.

McQuesten paid the hotel bill for Goodbody with his visa card. She looked at his face as he signed the chit. He looked at her out of the corner of his eye. He was sorry that he hadn't been able to enjoy her company last night. For Goodbody the important thing was that she was now safely with McQuesten. Goodbody seemed taken away and didn't feel comfortable with his mood. They left the lobby and walked through the front doors out to the narrow sidewalk. On the sidewalk people of all ages dressed in resort clothes were milling along with no apparent thought about where they were going. The sky was clear and the temperature was a perfect seventy degrees. Goodbody walked along in step with McQuesten. Her arm was hooked around his elbow. She turned her head for a quick glance behind them to see if they were being followed by some suspicious looking people. She was getting the hang of all this secret agent routine. Goodbody didn't want an Iraqi sneaking up from behind and grabbing her. She observed no one that caused her alarm. Again she glanced up at McQuesten. His face was totally focused on the business at hand.

Salih and Eta were one hundred feet down the sidewalk learning against the sedan lost in conversation. They had no idea McQuesten and Goodbody were walking toward them. They appeared like two lovers enjoying their honeymoon, oblivious to the world around them. Salih was wondering how much of his bounty from McQuesten he'd spend on Eta in Paris.

*   *   *

Abbas knew his career with the Iraqi private bank was finished. He felt confident there was enough money in his Swiss bank account to live for several years. Before going to Zurich, he had some personal scores to settle with Salih, the American prisoner, plus Ms. Goodbody, if he could find them. Abbas called the remaining security guards to the garage for a meeting. Abbas dug down deep inside and mentally prepared to give the guards a pep talk. This was, perhaps, his last time to be with them, he thought. He needed to concentrate to get his points made at this meeting with the guards. His mind was at odds because he was also thinking about Switzerland. The guards stood around Abbas looking intent, as he began to address them:

"Our man Salih and his French mistress have betrayed us. For this treason they must die. He is in league with the American CIA agent. We must find them and make them pay with their lives. Are you men with me? Say yes, if you are ready to follow my orders." The guards didn't respond immediately, but looked at each other and then answered, "We are with you, sir."

Abbas knew all the guards were Sunni tribal stock from north of Baghdad. He felt sure he could count on their loyalty, at least long enough to find Salih and the other two trouble makers.

"Two of you will drive me toward the Nice airport to search for the traitors. Everyone else will remain here and watch over things. I think the traitors may attempt to fly out of Nice rather than risk driving through France. We shall be looking for them traveling in our other sedan," said Abbas as he motioned to the two guards to start moving. He pumped his fist in the direction of the remaining guards.

*   *   *

Ramsey stood in the Nice airport Operations office, calling his old naval academy buddy who commanded the destroyer anchored four thousand yards out into the Bay.

"I may need your assistance to rescue a CIA officer and several agents who are working for us. Can you have your chopper on stand-by alert for the next twelve hours? I'm not sure if we'll need you, but we could require an emergency rescue pick-up. Following that, then a delivery to the Nice airport," said Ramsey.

The commanding officer, Commander E. Stanley listened to Ramsey.

"Okay, none of this will be a problem. We already have permission from the French port authority to launch our chopper on SAR missions while in port. I'll have our men wind up the chopper and take a spin around the Bay for some practice. Call us if you need us. Our men need some excitement, over."

"Roger, out," said Ramsey.

*   *   *

Iron Hand and Goodbody walked out of La Villa Juanaise Hotel, after paying her bill for the evening stay. Salih and Etta were seen leaning against the sedan about one-half a block away, engrossed in lover's conversation, totally oblivious to people walking along the sidewalk.

Iron Hand and Goodbody walked along the crowded sidewalk and came up to the sedan. Iron Hand kept checking behind and around the street doorways before entering the car. He didn't feel totally comfortable walking around the streets. He assumed that Abbas, his guards and informers were lurking everywhere around Juan les-Pins.

"Is everything under control?" asked Iron Hand.

"Yes. We are ready to get moving," said Salih.

"Very well, drive to the Nice airport. It should take us about fifteen minutes to get there in this traffic," said Iron Hand.

Salih and Etta climbed into the front seat with Iron Hand and Goodbody going into the back seat. As the sedan pulled into traffic, Salih noticed the other sedan owned by the bank traveling toward them from the opposite direction. It was moving slowly, as if the occupants were watching the crowds and traffic, looking for them.

"Everyone down," said Salih as he covered up his face with a city map that he had been reading moments before. Salih knew instinctively that Abbas had seen them when the other bank sedan rolled by them. Salih jammed on the accelerator before any of the guards could get to his car. Abbas ordered his guards to turn around in the street and follow Salih. One of Abbas's guards jumped out of the car and raced on foot after Salih's sedan to keep his eyes on its movements.

Salih drove on to highway N7 and pushed the car to the speed limit, ducking in and out of lanes to confuse their pursuers. As they rolled along, going east past road signs for Antibes, Fort Carre, and la Brague, Salih maneuvered onto A8 and sped toward the Aeroport de Nice-Cote d' Azur.

"Take the next turn left," ordered Iron Hand, as he glanced out the rear window. "That will take us north toward Biot. We can use several narrow, less traveled roads and lose these guys in the roads north of A8."

Iron Hand kept looking out the rear window and didn't see the sedan that contained the Iraqis. Of course, didn't necessarily mean they weren't close-by.

"Follow the sign ahead toward the golf course. Maybe we can lose these turkeys in one of the buildings or maintenance garages on the golf course," said Iron Hand as he thought that the golf fairways would give the chopper from the navy destroyer plenty of room for a landing. There was a small bridge over the Brague River and then the road led them into the golf course driveway.

"This is good. Let's get out and hide this car behind that building over there. We'll take on these guys here if we're forced into a shoot out. I'm getting tired of running away from these people," said Iron Hand as he grabbed Goodbody's hand and pulled her along toward the maintenance building. So far, no golf course employees had asked them who they were and what they were doing. After a few minutes however, a man wearing a golf tournament volunteer uniform came around the building. He looked curiously at the four people and asked,

"Are you here for the tournament?"

"What tournament?" answered McQuesten.

"Our club is sponsoring a two-day event with a golf exhibition of European PGA professionals plus a pro/am program later this afternoon," said the volunteer.

"Yes, we are here for the pro/am program. Our clubs will be coming along shortly. Please direct us to the clubhouse," said McQuesten who surprised himself that he could ad-lib his way into the golf tournament without any problems.

"Just walk up that path behind you. You'll see it on the left," said the volunteer.

McQuesten, Goodbody, Salih and Etta started up the pathway not knowing what to expect. The important point was to keep moving from Abbas and his men, who were probably not far behind them and prepared to kill them. Soon they were mixing with golfers and spectators milling around the clubhouse grounds. It gave McQuesten and party and opportunity to blend into the crowd. McQuesten knew this couldn't go on forever,so he began plotting his next move. Perhaps the two empty golf carts parked next to the official's tent could be commandeered. The carts had important looking official stickers on the wind shield announcing to the crowd that they were reserved for use by tournament officials.

"Let's walk over by those golf carts," McQusten said to his crew. They walked casually and settled into the seats. The keys were in the carts and ready to roll.

A young volunteer who looked like a typical bag-boy started walking toward the four visitors. McQuesten dug into his pocket and came up with a twenty dollar bill and pressed it into the young man's hand. The bag-boy smiled, turned away and walked back to the club house.

"Come on. Let's drive down this cart path and out to the course," said McQuesten. The two golf carts went down the path at high speed and were soon well away from the clubhouse reception area. McQuesten figured they were about one-half mile away with still no sign of Abbas and his men. McQuesten spotted an unattended SUV with the name of the golf club painted on the door. He drove up next to the SUV in his golf cart and saw the keys in the ignition. The driver was no where to be seen. McQuesten pulled the Officials Use Only tag from the golf cart and scribbled a note. He signed it and left if on the golf cart driver's seat. The note said, "Sorry I have to borrow this SUV. It will be returned later."

"Okay everyone, this is our chance to duck out of here and get back to the Nice airport," said McQuesten. They piled into the SUV with McQuesten driving down the road back toward highways N8 and N7. The road was lined with expensive homes that were undoubtedly owned by wealthy corporate executives and famous people. It was good to know that not everyone in Juan les-Pins was a tourist staying in hotels and leased villas. Well-groomed trees lined small ponds along the roadway that were full of water lilies. This made the scene as complete as an old master's water color painting. The French flag was flying from several of the homes. The scenery was so beautiful that Goodbody was hard pressed to remember she was running for her life.

*　　　　　*　　　　　*

Major Zabari deplaned and walked to the Nice airport customs office, dressed as a typical Iraqi business man in his dark suit, carrying a black attache' briefcase. Zabari had been well schooled by his Iraqi instructors how to act while going through a customs check point.

"Passport, please," said the woman customs agent.

"Certainly," said Zabari as he smiled and beamed at the woman.

"What is your reason for coming to Juan les-Pins?" asked the woman.

"Pleasure and vacationing," said Zabari.

"Do you have anything to declare?"

"No, nothing at this time."

"Very well, enjoy your stay in France," said the customs official.

Zabari hadn't brought luggage to hold a change of clothing. He did not plan on being in Juan les-Pins or Cannes more than twenty-four hours. He was supremely confident that he could perform his assignment in a matter of hours, contact the pilots, and be flying back to Baghdad.

Zabari got to a telephone and called the Iraqi bank in Cannes. A lady answered the telephone after two rings,

"La Compagnie Financiere Iraqi Banque, Cannes," said the French woman.

"Bonjour Mademoiselle, Je m'appelle Major Zabari de Baghdad. Ou sont mes amis Director Abbas et Salih? Parlez-vous anglais? Tres bien, merci. Et vous?"

"I'd like to speak to them."

"Neither of these gentlemen is here at the moment. Please hold while I connect you with a security guard," said the French woman.

Zabari thought for a moment; what is going on at the bank? There is only a security guard to speak with me? A soft voice came on the line.

"May I help you with something?" said the nervous guard who was not accustomed to speaking with bank officials from Baghdad.

"Yes, this Major Zabari from the Presidential Guard in Baghdad. I want to speak with Director Abbas or Salih. Please tell me where they are. It is important that I find them immediately." Zabari could tell from the guard's voice he was uncomfortable discussing Abbas and Salih. He wondered how much more he could have learned from this guard if he had pushed him a little harder.

"Sir, neither of the men you seek is here. Another security guard and I are the only men here in the bank. Director Abbas has been gone for about three hours. He recently contacted me and said he was near the Nice airport. He is looking for Salih and two foreigners. That is all I can tell you at this time, sir," said the security guard who was obviously nervous about his situation. "Would you like me to relay any message to Director Abbas, sir?"

"No, but I am also at the Nice airport. I will look for Director Abbas and Salih while I am here. There is no message. What type of car are they driving?"

"Sir, Director Abbas is in the bank's Mercedes sedan which is dark blue, four doors with tinted glass windows. Salih is also driving a similar car," said the security guard.

"Very well, thank you for your information. I will talk to you again later," said Zabari as he hung up the telephone. He walked to the curb side and looked around the airport parking lot but saw no four door Mercedes that matched the description given by the security guard. He retraced his path and walked up to a car rental booth to obtain transportation. He decided that a conservative convertible would be right for his short mission in Cannes.

The guard, Abdul, sat looking at the telephone. He tried to remember everything about the conversation he had just finished with the man from Baghdad.

"Abdul, who were you were talking to, some bank client?" said Ghazi, the other guard who was also nervous about being alone, protecting the entire bank.

"No, the man said he was from Baghdad and that his name was Zabari. I believe he said he was in the Presidential

Guard. A major in the Presidential Guard is what he said, I believe," said Abdul.

"My God," said Ghazi, "That man is a rumored hit-man for Saddam, supposedly Saddam's favorite assassin. I've heard some of the other guards speak of him."

"We'd better warn Director Abbas that this man has called the bank and that he's in Nice," said Abdul.

"I don't know," said Ghazi. "It's trouble either way."

"I'm going to call Director Abbas on the radio tele-phone. You can leave if you don't want to be part of what I'm going to do," said Abdul.

"I'm not sure we should call Abbas, but I'm going to stay here with you," said Ghazi.

Abdul tightened up his lips, nodded to Ghazi, and di-aled Abbas's special telephone number.

Abbas answered the car telephone and listened to his loyal Sunni guard Abdul relate his conversation with Major Zabari from Baghdad. As he put down the telephone his hand was shaking and sweat rolled down from his arm pits. Now he knew his time was limited because Saddam's long arm of retribution was reaching out for him. Abbas looked at his driver and said, "Pull over at the next opportunity and park. I need a few moments to think."

As the bank sedan pulled up into a small picnic area surrounded by trees, Abbas got out of the car and walked about ten paces and then returned to his car door which he had left open. He repeated this pattern of pacing several times. He then got back into the car and slammed the door closed. The driver had left the car running and the air conditioning felt good on Abbas's face. He was obviously planning his next move, which meant a quick trip to Zurich in a rental car. Fortunately, he had had the good sense to bring along his passport and some francs when he left the bank.

"Sir, an SUV just drove by going back toward the airport; I am sure the American prisoner was driving the car with the woman from the bank sitting next to him in the front seat," said the security guard.

"Pull around and chase them. If we can overtake them we will force them off the road and dispose of them once and for all," said Abbas; he then added, "If this turns out the way you said, I will reward you well for being so observant."

The guard checked his rear view mirror for traffic, saw none, wheeled the sedan around in a sharp turn, gunned the engine and was soon speeding down the road. In a matter of minutes, Abbas had the SUV in his view. "Don't alarm them by getting too close," said Abbas, adding, "We want to surprise them. We will trap them, leaving no opportunity for escape."

McQuesten remembered that there was a soccer field about two miles down this road, thinking it would be a good pick-up point for the helicopter from the Navy ship. No need for this soccer field now; with the SUV they could drive right to the Nice airport, thought McQuesten,

Suddenly his plans changed when he saw a sedan getting a little too close to him coming around the last curve in the road.

"Silah, do you recognize the car and driver behind us?" asked McQuesten.

"Yes, that is one of our bank security guards. I believe that Abbas is in the front seat with him."

"My God, how can we ever shake these guys," said McQuesten. Now the soccer field became an important new destination. In a few moments the driveway to the soccer field would be directly in front of them. A decision would have to be made immediately. McQuesten swung the wheel of the SUV and drove onto the soccer field which was empty of activity. McQuesten pulled to a stop and reached for his Beretta pistol. He looked at Goodbody and said, "Do you think you can use that nine-millimeter gun in your purse?"

"I can sure try. I'm a fast learner."

Silah and Etta were panicked in the back seat. Silah mumbled, "What's going to happen? Will I be killed?"

McQuesten looked back and said,

"Try to relax. They won't charge this car because they must know we have weapons. Get down as low as you can on the car floor and stay there. There could be some gun-play." Etta became frightened and looked at Silah with terror in her eyes.

*   *   *

Zabari had been studying his map of Juan les-Pins for ten minutes when he decided to drive up the small roads that would take him north of the main highways. He had already driven slowly through the airport parking lots. He had not seen any cars matching the description given to him by the Iraqi bank security guard.

The Juan les-Pins Affair

8

Zabari drove his car west on N7 toward Cros de Cagnes, Villeneuve, Loubet-Plage and La Brague. He followed a hunch and drove the car down N7, which guided him toward his prey. It was like a hunter's perceptive notion locking on his prey. Fighter pilots refer to this as target fixation when they bore in on the enemy. When Zabari came to the road sign for Biot, he turned north. He thought about the beauty of the surrounding area and the lovely homes nestled throughout the hills.

As he cruised along the road, not knowing exactly where he was going, his eye caught sight of a dark sedan parked on a soccer field that matched the description given to him by the bank guard. He braked, checked the rear view mirror, found no traffic behind him, and eased off the road. He turned his attention to the dark sedan four hundred yards away and the two men standing next to it. He had played his hunch perfectly: there was Abbas and a guard, each holding a pistol, walking toward the gray SUV parked nearby on the soccer field.

Zabari gunned his car across the road and steered directly at Abbas and his guard. As the car accelerated across the soccer field, he pulled his gun from his shoulder holster and released the safety catch. Relying on his excellent marksmanship, he braked the car just enough to steady his aim. With his left arm braced on the door window track, he squeezed the trigger for his first shot. The bullet found its target and Abbas slumped to the ground, but not before he had turned to see the driver of the approaching car pointing a weapon. The bullet creased Abbas on his right shoulder, inflicting a nonfatal wound, but still with enough force to knock him down and cause great pain. Abbas's security guard, being focused on the SUV, didn't know how to react. Realizing that Abbas was wounded, he fell to the ground and prepared to fire at the driver of the convertible, if it moved closer. The guard called to Abbas,

"Sir, are you able to speak? Can you hear me?" Abbas was writhing in pain and struggled to find the words to answer,

"I am wounded and bleeding, but not yet ready to die." At this point, Abbas fought his pain, rolled over, raised his weapon, pointed it toward the convertible and fired twice. The bullets carried high over the head of Zabari and lodged in a tree branch twenty yards in the background. Abbas was sure that the man who shot him was the Baghdad assassin the Sunni bank guard had described. How the assassin had tracked them down was a mystery that Abbas couldn't fathom. Abbas yelled to his guard,

"If you can see the man in the convertible, shoot and kill him before he kills us!"

Of course Zabari heard Abbas shouting orders to his guard. Zabari then yelled to the guard,

"I'm not here to fight with you. Only Abbas and Salih have been ordered to die by Saddam. Throw down your gun and walk toward my car."

The Sunni guard was torn with indecision. He remembered his oath to Abbas. His loyalty to Abbas was firm and true, but he didn't want to die at the hands of this stranger. He wondered if he stood up, dropped his weapon as this man ordered, would the stranger shoot him down like a dog. He froze with fear and hugged the ground.

Inside the SUV, McQuesten and Goodbody heard the shots and the loud voices of men yelling behind them. It was time to call for reinforcements. McQuesten pulled out his cell phone and punched the button for activation. While waiting for the cell phone to link up with a satellite, he fumbled through his wallet to find the special number to connect with the Navy Captain. The cell phone finally came to life and McQuesten punched out the numbers for the

Captain of the US Naval destroyer anchored four miles due south in the Baie des Anges. Ramsey had said a helicopter rescue could probably be arranged. Somehow the electronics worked and his call was completed. McQuesten sighed and thought, "Thank God the NRO satellites were on the job."

"This is Captain Stanley, USS Cole. What can I do for you?"

"This is McQuesten, Captain US Navy and CIA officer approximately four miles due north from your position. I believe Brad Ramsey briefed you about me. We need a priority rescue effort immediately. We are under fire from killers using small arms in a soccer field north of E80 highway. We are pinned down in a gray SUV. Anything you can do would be appreciated. There are four people who need to be lifted out of this situation, over."

"Roger your last, Captain. We will launch our chopper immediately. Suggest you start flashing your headlights on the SUV in two minutes. This will guide them to your location. Stanley, roger, out."

Goodbody listened to McQuesten and asked,

"Are we going to get out of this fix alive?"

McQuesten looked into her blue eyes and knew she was very worried. He tried to bolster her confidence, saying, "I think so. Just hang in there. Get out your gun and don't be afraid to shoot someone sneaking up behind us. The navy ship in the harbor is sending in a chopper to pick us up if we can hold out here."

"I remember the last chopper rescue that your man Ramsey set up for us. That guy got lost. Does this chopper pilot know what he's doing?" Goodbody questioned with a pleading look on her face.

"We have to hope so. Do you think you can handle that gun in your purse?" asked McQuesten as the mood in the SUV began to get tense.

"Just get it ready to fire. Where is the safety? Put a bullet in the chamber and set it for automatic. Then I'll be okay, I think," said Goodbody as her eyes flashed with excitement.

McQuesten took the nine-millimeter and pumped back the slide action, which slammed a bullet into the chamber. He then switched off the safety. When he handed it back he said, "Here you go. This weapon is ready to be fired. Hold the gun with both hands. Just point at your target and squeeze the trigger."

McQuesten didn't expect Goodbody to actually kill anyone but she might scare them off while they ran to the chopper. Hopefully, the pilot was going to find them. McQuesten was impressed with the way Goodbody held the pistol. Salih and Etta were still lying flat on the back seat floor of the SUV, and not talking. Salih knew there was an assassin from Baghdad less than one hundred feet away who had been sent to kill him. The promised fifty thousand bucks from McQuesten didn't seem like a lot of money right now. Etta was about to break into tears. She had had no idea this was how her afternoon would be spent - praying for her life. The fast party life she had hoped to find didn't include getting involved in a shoot-out.

Zabari began moving the car toward Abbas. He drove slowly, keeping his pistol aimed at Abbas in case he was playing possum. He was also keeping one eye on Abbas's guard. He would fire at either man who moved. The guard had been given a chance to surrender, thought Zabari, but had chosen not to follow his orders. Now he was ready to kill him, too.

Abbas could see the convertible creeping toward him and he moved a little to his left to get a better shot at the driver. Even though his body was racked with pain, Abbas steadied his gun with both hands and squeezed off two shots that hit the car, but it still continued to come toward him. Why didn't his guard shoot at the car? thought Abbas. At this point, the guard raised himself up and squeezed off a shot at the convertible. The bullet went through the wind shield and shattered glass into the front seat. Zabari wheeled the car toward the guard and fired twice. The guard fell in his tracks and moaned his last, after the bullets cut into his chest.

Abbas rolled over and screamed in pain as his shoulder bounced off the turf. Zabari swung his car around and headed directly toward Abbas. Abbas had counted his shots and knew he had four bullets left in his pistol. He was determined to use all of them to kill this Baghdad assassin. As the car came closer, Abbas spread down on the turf to give the driver the smallest target. Abbas had his gun ready to fire but he was determined not to panic and waste his last bullets.

Zabari was sure the guard was dead, so now Abbas became his only focus. He would not allow himself to mess up this assignment. Abbas was going to die, now. He moved the car slowly toward the wounded Abbas, with his arm resting on the window track and the pistol ready. He zeroed in the gun sight on Abbas. He squeezed the trigger and fired a single shot. Abbas felt the bullet tear through the same shoulder that had already been hit. With this second wound, the pain exploded in his body and holding his gun on target became next to impossible. Fighting to hold his aim, Abbas fired twice and saw the car stop momentarily, but then it moved again toward him. The driver fired again and the bullet tore through Abbas' chest. He dropped his gun and rolled over, dead.

The car moved closer to Abbas's body and Zabari fired two quick shots into Abbas' prone body to ensure that he was dead.

Zabari did not know that Salih was inside the SUV but he assumed, correctly, that someone of interest was hiding inside the vehicle. Why else would Abbas and his guard be attacking it? He drove his convertible around to the back of the SUV and fired one shot into each of the rear tires. No one was going to drive away from him with two flat tires. He considered firing two slugs into the fuel tank to get the gasoline burning. That would certainly force the occupants from the SUV and he could pick-off the man ordered to die.

Zabari decided to stop and figure his best way to approach the people in the SUV. He shouted out, "If Salih is inside the van, I want him. He's the only person I want."

Salih raised himself up from the back seat and looked at McQuesten,. He was totally terrified as he said, "You aren't going to force me out of this van, are you? This man will kill me."

"Relax. No one is going to leave this SUV until the chopper is on the soccer field. We've got this guy outgunned right now. I'm guessing the chopper will also have men with guns to back us up. Stay down back there with Etta until I tell you what to do," ordered McQuesten.

Salih nodded his head in agreement to the orders from McQuesten. There was never a thought in his mind of doing anything but what McQuesten ordered. Etta continued to look frightened and was in near total panic mode.

McQuesten heard a chopper in the sky but couldn't see it. He looked at Goodbody and said, "Start flashing the head lights. The chopper crew is looking for a signal from us. That will guide them in here."

McQuesten looked in the rear view mirror and saw the driver of the convertible sitting in the car. McQuesten slowly opened the door and eased out of the SUV. He hugged the side of the SUV and edged back toward the rear. His Beretta was drawn and ready to shoot if the driver of the car made any threatening moves.

Zabari had reloaded his weapon and jammed an extra clip of bullets into his pant pocket. He could see someone was sneaking back from the driver's side of the van. He gunned his car and drove around the opposite side to get a look at the passenger in the front seat. He noticed an attractive woman in the front seat, but she didn't cause him to feel threatened. He thought to himself, "I don't have to shoot her."

Goodbody saw the convertible coming around to her side of the SUV so she pulled the nine millimeter pistol up and pointed it out the window toward the driver. She knew she couldn't miss the car at this close range. She planned to hold her fire until the driver made some threatening move. Then her reflexes took over and she squeezed off one shot at the car. The driver reacted by ducking down, gunning the car past her door and firing two shots at the SUV. The slugs went past Goodbody and hit the front windshield which exploded into thousands of glass bits. Goodbody then pointed her gun, squeezed the trigger, and emptied her pistol into the car. She wasn't sure if she even hit the car, let alone the driver. The gun kicked every time it fired a round so it was difficult for her to steady the gun.

McQuesten retraced his steps to the front of the van and leveled his Beretta at the driver of the convertible as it went by the front of the SUV.

Zabari was surprised at the gun fire he received from the SUV. He turned his car to the right, looped around and made a quick drive-by pass toward the right side of the van where Goodbody was sitting in the passenger seat. She was attempting to fire her gun but it was empty. She ducked down and began to pray. Zabari fired two shots into the door behind the passenger seat and one slug found its way to Salih's chest. He moaned with pain and blood began to spill over Etta. Goodbody leaned over the seat and tried to comfort Salih and calm down Etta who was losing her cool from all the guns firing and blood gushing from Salih's wound.

McQuesten came around the front of the van and fired his Beretta pistol at the convertible until it was empty. Zabari spun the car around and drove off one hundred yards away and stopped.

Salih was in great pain as the bullet wound to his chest continued to bleed. His face was turning pale and his breathing was labored. Etta looked at McQuesten and said,

"This man is near death and I believe that the killer will go to the bank and murder everyone who is there. Please let me use your cell-phone to warn my friends back at the bank. These women have families and they need to leave before this madman goes there."

McQuesten didn't have a problem with Etta calling her work-mates at the bank. She was probably correct that this hired killer would go to the bank. Goodbody tugged at McQuesten, signaled a thumbs-up while nodding approval to

Etta's request for the cell-phone. McQuesten reached into his pocket for his phone and handed it to Etta.

Moments later Etta was talking to Louise who gasped at the horror of Abbas' death and Silah's terrible wounds. Etta rambled on about the situation and ended by saying, "I think the killer will come to the bank after he leaves us. Please leave the bank building at once and go home. No one can tell what he will do. Comprenez-vous? A tout a l'heure. Au revoir." Etta handed the cell-phone to McQuesten and burst into tears.

*   *   *

At the Iraqi bank, Louise sat at her desk trying to assimilate what Etta told her. She called to Margot. "Etta has called me. Abbas is dead and Silah is near death with a bullet in his chest. She believes the killer may be on his way here. Our lives could be in danger. I believe we should gather our things and leave the bank immediately."

The two remaining security bank guards, Abdul and Ghazi, looked disorganized after the news from Louise settled in their minds. Each man stared into the other's eyes and came to the same conclusion. With Abbas dead and Silah near death they were released from their loyalty oath. It was now everyman for himself. Relief flooded over them.

Their first thought was to get any loose cash from the desks of Abbas and Salih. The two French women had left the building, so there would be no witnesses to anything they did inside the bank. They rushed to the second floor and ransacked the manager's desks for cash. Each desk contained a cash box which the guards knew held large Euro notes and American currency. They stuffed the money into their pockets. They carefully wiped their finger prints off the cash boxes and replaced them in the desks. They then walked down to the first floor and locked all the side doors. As they left the bank by the front door, the two guards placed the front door keys in the potted palms beside the doors. The two men walked out the front gates and down the sidewalk. As they made their way into town, Ghazi said to Abdul,

"I believe we should go to Seurat's restaurant and get some food and drinks. We can plan our next move from there. I think our work here is finished. I am only concerned about staying alive. Perhaps Seurat can give us an idea about where to hide from this killer sent by Baghdad."

As Abdul walked along the sidewalk, he tried to absorb what Ghazi was saying, finally reacting; he said,

"You are right. Why should we stand and fight for the bank when our managers have been murdered by one of Saddam's killers? I have nothing in Iraq. These people will only try to blame us for what has happened. I can live in France and maybe work for Seurat, or someone like him."

Ghazi, ever the optimist, said,

"Look at it this way; the population in France is twenty percent Muslim. We can blend in and the authorities will never know about us. Seurat is getting old. Perhaps we can buy out his gambling book racket and run it ourselves. There are many Muslims who would do business with us. How does this sound to you?"

Abdul looked at Ghazi and smiled in agreement. The two Iraqis continued walking down the street confident that they were on the way to the next chapter in their lives.

*   *   *

The navy chopper was hovering overhead while McQuesten signaled to the pilot that he had arrived at the proper landing position. The chopper landed and a sailor armed with an M-16 rifle jumped out to provide cover fire. With his flank covered, McQuesten returned to the SUV and pulled Goodbody out of the front seat. They ran hand in hand to the chopper.

"Hey, what took you guys so long to call for the cavalry?" asked Ramsey with a big smile on his face.

"What are you doing here?" asked Goodbody as she struggle to get fastened into a chopper seat.

"I asked the Captain to pick me up just before your call came through for help. We were already to take off so I just came along," said Ramsey proudly.

After Goodbody was securely inside the chopper, McQuesten returned for Salih and Etta. McQuesten picked up Salih and carried him to the chopper. Etta ran alongside McQuesten and tried to shield herself from the killer in the car. In less than three minutes McQuesten's party was aboard the chopper. It lifted off the soccer field and headed for the destroyer and medical attention for Salih.

McQuesten checked Salih's condition and turned to the pilot, "Radio the ship to have a medic team standing by. We have one badly wounded passenger."

"It doesn't look good for the Iraqi," said a corpsman.

"Do the very best you can for the man. This guy saved my life."

The corpsman continued to work on Salih's body. Stopping the bleeding was the most important job. He tried to make Salih comfortable. He paused for a moment, looked up at McQuesten and said,

"I'll keep you posted how he's doing."

The Juan les-Pins Affair

9

When the Navy chopper lifted off the soccer field Zabari watched from a distance in his bullet-riddled car. The opportunity to complete the assassination plot had been taken away by the Americans. Zabari's face snarled with disgust as he drove back toward the airport. He sorted through his remaining options to finish his mission. He knew that failure was never rewarded by Saddam Hussein.

He was sure that the helicopter would take the passengers back to the airport and a waiting plane. If he could get to the airport and somehow find their plane, he might have just a small window of time to kill Salih. Somewhere on the airport runway there would be a business jet waiting for the people in the helicopter. Therefore, the only problem would be to figure out which plane was waiting for these people.

While in route to the airport, he pulled his cell phone from his pocket and dialed the secret telephone numbers of the General at the headquarters of the Presidential Guard in Baghdad. Zabari was always anxious to report any partial success to his senior officers. He knew that the General liked to pass along good reports to Saddam's office when there was a contract being executed. There was nothing like good news to build his image back in Baghdad. Zabari waited for the call to go through. Finally the telephone was answered by a General's aid. Zabari requested and got an immediate hook-up with the General.

"Abbas has been eliminated. The number two man, Salih, is probably mortally wounded, but I can't confirm his condition at this time," said Zabari to the General of the Presidential Guard.

"This is a good report but you must finish your assignment. Also, we have received information from our spies that the woman from Denmark is being aided by a CIA Officer. They have probably been working together from the beginning. If you kill these two people, you will be doing a great service for Saddam. Do you feel this is possible?"

"Yes, I think it may be possible to eliminate all of them. I have seen these people and feel highly confident. I will not fail Saddam. Please allow me to contact you soon when I have more good news." Zabari realized that with the orders to kill these additional people his reputation could soar to even greater heights in Baghdad.

"Praise Allah," said the General as he signed off.

*   *   *

Immediately after chopper lifted off the soccer field, a crewman examined Salih and leaned close to McQuesten to talk over the noise from the chopper blades.

"Sir, this man will be history if he doesn't get to a hospital. Our ship can't give him the medical attention he needs. There's an emergency hospital with a landing pad near-by. We could drop him there. At least, there he might have a fighting chance."

Without hesitation, McQuesten answered,

"Tell the pilot to fly to the hospital. Also, tell him to radio ahead that we are bringing a gun-shot victim."

"Yes, sir," said the crewman, who immediately pulled himself up to the pilot's position.

McQuesten glanced toward Etta and nodded. She was fighting back tears. The time dragged on but Salih continued clinging to life. Finally, they arrived on the roof landing pad and the emergency staff removed Salih from the helicopter and disappeared into the building. Ramsey jumped out of the chopper and ran into the building to give the necessary information to the hospital staff. In a short time Ramsey returned and flashed a thumb's up sign to McQuesten.

"I hope we got him here in time," said Etta.

McQuesten looked at Etta and said,

"He's pretty tough. I'll bet he makes it."

Etta looked at McQuesten and sat back in her seat. Her eyes, swelling up with tears, glanced back toward the hospital doors as she wondered if Salih was dead or alive.

*   *   *

Zabari drove to the airport and headed toward a maintenance hanger and general aviation flight operations center. He parked his shot-up car behind a fuel truck and walked quickly to the nearest building. For what ever reason there was little security around the area. He entered a door marked "Airport Personnel Only" and found the room deserted. There was a series of lockers and a clothes rack holding overalls for runway baggage handlers. Zabari found a clean suit of overalls and quickly donned them over his clothes. He walked outside and climbed into a baggage handling vehicle, started the engine and drove down the tarmac to begin his search for an executive jet plane preparing to depart with passengers. Traveling down the flight line of jets he noticed some activity around a white Lear jet. Its engines were turning over and the pilots had placed a small red carpet in front of the doorway. The pilots sat in the cockpit and were totally occupied running through their routine departure check lists.

Zabari drove his runway service vehicle up and stopped near the portside wing tip without attracting any attention. He reached down and picked up some paper work on a clipboard and busied himself so as to appear like he was part of the ground crew checking for baggage and fuel supplies. From all appearances he concluded that the passengers had not yet arrived, so his timing was perfect, if this was the plane that was going to carry his targets from Nice. As he faked studying the paperwork clipboard, he heard the blades of a helicopter circling overhead. He calmly

110

looked toward the sky and saw the same small US Navy military helicopter circling to make a landing hear the Lear jet. Zabari was very pleased with himself, since he gotten into position to kill these people without any trouble. His training and skill at organizing his thoughts was paying off for him. He pressed his hand against his pistol and made sure it was ready for use at a moments notice. Now it was just a matter of waiting until the passengers of the helicopter walked by his vehicle and he could shoot them down in the name of his leader, Saddam Hussein.

"What will happen to Salih?" asked Etta again.

"I hope he will recover from his wounds but right now his situation is doubtful. He lost a lot of blood and his condition is critical. It all depends on the skill of the surgeons," replied McQuesten.

Etta looked sad. She didn't know what to say at hearing this assessment of Salih's chances. "I'm not in love with Salih but I do feel sorry for him. I was just looking for some excitement when I started dating him. I never thought it would come to this." She slumped into her seat.

"There's nothing you can do right now. He's where he belongs. The doctors will save him if he's strong enough to survive the operation," said McQuesten as he noticed that Etta was taking the news fairly well.

"You have a decision to make, Etta. Do you want to come with us or do you want to stay here in Juan les-Pins?" said McQuesten.

"There really is nothing here for me. I do not want to go back to the bank. I feel that it's too dangerous for me now. I'll come with you. I'll get back to Paris somehow and pick up my life with my parents help. They will never believe what I've been through in such a short time," said Etta.

"Maybe we can arrange to drop you off at le Bourget in Paris. We'll be going on to Denmark, but I can speak to the pilots. It shouldn't be that big of a deal. Could you get to your home in Paris if I'm able to arrange for you to fly to Paris?" asked McQuesten.

"Yes, that would be wonderful. I'm sure I can get home from le Bourget without difficulty."

*   *   *

"Stand by for our landing on the runway," said the chopper pilot.

The Navy chopper landed fifty feet away from the Lear Jet. The door opened and Ramsey, McQuesten, Goodbody and Etta climbed out of the chopper and walked toward the Lear jet. The armed sailor with his carbine rifle preceded them from the chopper and looked around the plane. He visually checked out the baggage handler sitting in the vehicle but didn't feel he posed a threat.

"Do we have luggage somewhere that must come aboard this plane?" asked the sailor.

"No. We are traveling without luggage. Just four of us are going aboard the plane," answered McQuesten as he moved quickly, leading the way toward the jet.

McQuesten and company reached the jet plane and began climbing the ladder into the cabin. Zabari bided his time, waiting for the precise moment when he could shoot and not miss. His hand began to move toward his pistol but he hesitated for a few moments longer. Suddenly an idea came to him. He would wait until the passengers were inside the cabin, run up the ladder, get the drop on them and hijack the plane to Baghdad. He would deliver the dead bodies to Baghdad and get a hero's welcome from the Presidential Guard General. His glory would be everlasting. He would be a hero in the eyes of Saddam. It was a perfect plan. He felt that he was brilliant to think of it at this last moment.

Zabari watched carefully as the last man got into the cabin. He looked over his shoulder and saw the Navy chopper leaving the runway. He left the vehicle and walked carefully toward the ladder as though he was going to assist them in raising it into the plane. At the last moment, he pulled out his pistol and sprang up the ladder.

"Everyone be seated and no one will get hurt,' he shouted to the passengers.

Ramsey and McQuesten were startled and looked at each other while standing frozen next to their seats. The two women had already seated themselves and were shocked to see a man waving a pistol at them. McQuesten knew his Beretta was empty from his last encounter with this assassin. He berated himself for not reloading his weapon when he had the opportunity. Goodbody had also fired the last bullet from her gun. Their only hope was that perhaps Ramsey had a pistol that he could use to kill this madman. As Iron Hand and Ramsey began to seat themselves, the door from the cockpit area opened up and the co-pilot entered the cabin.

"What's going on here? Who are you? Get off this plane immediately," said the co-pilot in a strong voice. Zabari reacted by waving his pistol in the face of the co-pilot and ordered him to get back into his seat.

"I am taking command of this plane. Stay off the radio. Move and do what you are told," said Zabari.

When Zabari turned his head to confront the co-pilot McQuesten leaped from his seat and grabbed at Zabari's arm. It was just enough to distract Zabari and the co-pilot lurched toward Zabari and pushed him into McQuesten's body as he grabbed at the hand holding the pistol. Ramsey got out of his seat and jumped into the pile of the three men as they all struggled for control of the gunman. One shot went off and the bullet went through the open door into the sky. The sound of the gun caused Etta and Goodbody to scream, causing more confusion for the struggling men. By now the pilot of the plane was out of his seat and approached the pile of men fighting. He had his own pistol in hand. He realized what was happening. He hammered down hard on Zabari's head with his gun. Zabari was out cold from the blow to the back of his head. McQuesten picked up the assassin's pistol and handed it to Ramsey.

"Check out this pistol. Empty the magazine. We'll give it to the security people."

The assassin was then tied up with extra seat belts until the security people arrived. Ramsey and McQuesten dragged the unconscious Zabari from the plane and dumped him into the baggage service vehicle. Plane tie-down lines in the back seat of the service vehicle were used to further restrain the assassin, so he would have no opportunity to escape.

"My God, I thought we were goners," said Ramsey.

"Yes, this was a close call," answered McQuesten as he stared at the frozen face of Zabari. "I'm positive this is the same guy who was shooting at us back at the soccer field. I wonder how he got to the airport so quickly after we lifted off from the soccer field?"

Ramsey stood by the baggage service vehicle making sure there would be slip-ups answered, "He must have made up the time when we dropped Salih at the hospital. That was the time frame opening he used to get here ahead of us. Then he got lucky and guessed which jet was going to take us out,"

"That's exactly what happened."

"Airport security can turn this guy over to the Nice police. I'm anxious to leave Juan les-Pins," said Ramsey.

The Lear jet pilot radioed the control tower that a hijacking attempted had been foiled. Security personnel were dispatched immediately. Upon their arrival at the jet, the airport security personnel took control of the hijacker. The pilots finished their preflight check list, as the four passengers once again attempted to get settled in the plane.

*   *   *

The Lear jet taxied to the runway and lifted off the runway for Paris. The flight was smooth and without problems. During the flight Ramsey spoke with McQuesten.

"I have business in Paris with the Interpol hackers who siphoned the funds from the La Compagnie Financiere Iraqi Banque. I will also see that Etta gets to her home without any further incidents. This leaves you alone with Goodbody. Can you deal with that?" Ramsey asked with a smirk on his face.

"Yeah, it'll be tough, but I can handle it," said McQuesten with a smile, and then he added, "Will you please stop that kind of talk."

*   *   *

Jacques Murat settled back in a leather chair behind his desk on the second floor of his office in downtown Juan les-Pins. He heaved a sigh of relief, put his feet on his desk, and recalled the rumor his crime syndicate captain reported. The rumor on the street had it that the Iraqi bank in Cannes had been brought down by Interpol, with an assist by the American CIA. It hadn't taken long for these whispers to make the rounds in Juan les-Pins.

Murat had little sympathy for Saddam Hussein and the alleged losses he suffered at the hands of the two huge government agencies. However, it was unsettling that a big stream of money for his crime organization was gone. It was time to plan ways of extracting revenge.

Five years ago Murat had joined forces with the Russian crime syndicate in Marseilles that was controlled by Vladimir Zhukov. He knew he was expected to develop an action plan against Interpol and the CIA because they had cut into their profits. The retribution must be done so that nothing could be traced back to their crime organization. The Russian syndicate always played the game of pay-back against any organization that challenged their organization.

Murat knew that Interpol and local French police had left his crime organization alone for years because the crime family had helped the Allies defeat the Germans in 1944 and later rendered service to France in the 1960's during the Algerian War.

Murat's organized crime family was a conduit for money skimmed from Iraqi crude oil smuggled aboard

115

tankers that made regular deliveries to Marseilles. After becoming aligned with the Russian crime syndicate, his business had picked up substantially. The last few years had been particularly profitable. Now it appeared that this stream of kick-back money would dry up.

Murat had grown up in a large family, living along the Cote d' Azur in Toulon. His father worked on the docks and the fish wholesaling business. Once he was old enough to work he started as a kitchen helper, working in hotels along the French Riviera. He observed how the rich enjoyed their wealth. Gradually he worked his way into the crime family that controlled off-track racing betting parlors and protection rackets along the Cote d' Azur. Much later he became involved in the drug trade rackets as an enforcer.

On his thirty-fifth birthday, he had become a captain of the organized crime family in Juan les-Pins.

In the opinion of most women, the six foot two-inch Murat had elegance, class and style. He had become the business brain behind the crime empire on the Cote d' Azur. He used his good looks and sex appeal to get to the top in his crime family. Having observed how the rich excelled at living well, he made sure his office was striking and stunning. His office interiors were done in his favorite colors – black, silver and gray. Pictures and accessories were carefully chosen to let associates know he was the boss. He had married early in his life but the stress of his crime family business caused the marriage to fail.

Any action by someone who threatened his crime organization brought swift reaction by him, since he viewed these challenges as a direct attack against his leadership. Murat knew the importance of leading his men against anyone who caused trouble. He wasn't afraid of any Interpol agents or the American CIA. From time to time these people had to be reminded not to come after his organization.

The weapon of choice for Murat was always a Luger pistol from his private collection of handguns. His favorite pistol was a Swiss military 7.65 mm, chrome plated, with a four and three quarter inch barrel equipped with a silencer.

He also had several Luger P-08 pistols manufactured in 1938 that had been used by the German officer corps in WW II. Murat was not considered a trigger man in any sense of the word, but he was not reluctant to accompany his men when they settled scores with enemies.

After learning from informers that the men from the CIA had left Juan les-Pins the previous day, Murat knew he must send men to Denmark to kill the CIA officer and the bank informant who had provided the banking information about the money laundering ring. No one from the Iraqi bank expected Murat's crime syndicate to take any revenge because of the bank collapse. Murat did not expect any thanks from the Iraqis for the action he planned to initiate. For Murat, it was just a matter of honor and pay-back for the lack of respect. His men would hold him in higher esteem if they knew their leader had settled the score and made the trouble makers pay for disturbing their business in the Cote d' Azur. The only matter of concern now was how best to arrange the revenge plot.

Murat learned from his Paris contacts that they had easily established who had tipped off Interpol about their money laundering. After discovering the informant was a woman, he decided to go to Copenhagen and personally supervise ransacking her apartment and eliminating her. It would be a simple matter to make his revenge appear like a random crime. Murat decided to fly to Copenhagen with his best and most-trusted enforcer. It would be a two-man job. He called his assistant into his office.

"Raoul, arrange for a private plane to take me and Francois to Copenhagen. We will leave as soon as the arrangements are completed."

Raoul nodded and said, "Very good, sir. Will you and Francois be staying long in Copenhagen?" Raoul stood by the door waiting for his boss to answer.

"No. I don't expect to be there more than one day. In-struct the pilots to stand-by in Copenhagen to bring us back in the evening," said Murat as he toyed with a cigarette and looked out the window at a tree-line park across the street from his office. Murat's mind was busy fantasizing about the Danish woman who tipped off the authorities.

*　　　　*　　　　*

McQuesten and Goodbody landed at the Copenhagen airport in time for dinner to celebrate their safe return from their adventure in southern France. While sitting in the plane Goodbody had made the personal decision not to return to her job in the small banking office near the Stroget. She planned to resign from the bank unless they offered her a good job in the downtown headquarters. She was rehearsing what she would say to her department head the next day.

Since the two adventurers were traveling light, they were able to clear customs easily. They were quickly standing on the curbside looking for transportation. As the two stood by waiting for a taxi, Goodbody looked at McQuesten and said,

"I don't want to be alone tonight in my apartment."

"I'm glad to hear you say that. I feel the same way. Let's have dinner at The Plaza Hotel. We can wind-down and talk about this," said McQuesten feeling a little uncomfortable about making a play for Goodbody after her comment. "I have a small suite which is very comfortable. You could have your own bed so you would be safe. Tomorrow we can go to your apartment and see how things are there," said McQuesten, as he wondered just what was going on in Goodbody's mind.

"This sounds good. Let's go have dinner. I need a glass of wine too. It will be nice to relax over a good meal and not have to worry about an Iraqi hounding me," said Goodbody as she hooked her arm around McQuesten.

They walked over to a taxi and climbed into the back seat. McQuesten could feel the warmth of her body as they settled into the back seat of the taxi. Goodbody looked at McQuesten and said,

"I'm so tired of these clothes. I think I'll buy something to wear from The Plaza Hotel boutique. Why don't you come with me? I'm dying to use my charge card again."

"Okay, I'll tag along. Maybe I could pick up a new shirt too," said McQuesten, who was going along with her to be agreeable. He then remembered that he had a suitcase full of clean clothes that he had placed in storage with the hotel bell captain prior to his trip to France. McQuesten thought to himself, I can always use a new good shirt for casual dressing. As the taxi moved through the traffic, Goodbody closed her eyes and McQuesten relaxed and surveyed the buildings as they rolled along the crowded streets heading for their hotel.

*   *   *

The French gangsters rode along the highway toward Copenhagen in their rented black C 70 Volvo. They had departed Nice at sunrise and experienced an uneventful trip. Murat had his Luger pistol and an extra clip of bullets tucked into his belt holster. Francois was armed with a Walther HP automatic 9.00 mm parabellam semi-automatic pistol with an eight round clip. Francois was an excellent driver, having driven many miles around the winding roads of the Cote d' Azur for the crime family. The trip into Copenhagen from the airport took thirty minutes.

Their plan was simple. They had been supplied with the address of the woman who had tipped off Interpol. They would go directly to her apartment and eliminate her. If she wasn't in her apartment, they would ransack her belongings and wait nearby for her return. After she saw the ransacked apartment, she'd undoubtedly be upset, frightened and nervous. They assumed she would hurriedly leave and then the two Frenchmen would follow her and kill her. If her CIA officer bodyguard was in her company they would also eliminate him. Afterward they would immediately return to the airport for their flight back to France.

The two mobsters from Juan les-Pins had received photographs of Goodbody from their Paris contacts. The pictures were taken from the Paris apartment of Gertrude Arnaud. She had been found dead by a maid in her small apartment on the left bank. Arnaud had been shot several times at close range with a small caliber gun. Goodbody's name had been written on the back of each photo taken of her on a street in Copenhagen. After the bank money-laundering scheme was blown in Copenhagen, Arnaud managed to flee back to Paris. Arnaud apparently had been secretly enthralled with Goodbody's appearance and brought along Goodbody's photos.

*   *   *

McQuesten and Goodbody awoke from a long sleep after making love the evening before. Goodbody looked at McQuesten and said, with a sly smile,

"You are my first American man with whom I have made love."

"Am I different than European men?" McQuesten asked without thinking. Suddenly he thought perhaps he shouldn't have asked the question.

"Yes, you are different. I would say, better than the men I've known before," she answered and playfully pushed at him with her hand.

"Well, it's nice to know I'm good at something," said McQuesten with a smile and small laugh.

With this, Goodbody reached over and kissed McQuesten again. She then jumped from the bed and stood naked in front of the mirror. She played with her hair for a few moments and then walked to the shower. She quietly closed the door and turned on the shower. McQuesten pulled up the bed sheets, reached for the TV remote and searched the television channels for CNN.

After resisting the temptation of Goodbody's clean body, McQuesten suggested a leisurely breakfast to which

Goodbody readily agreed. The two warriors refreshed but still tired from their adventure in Juan les-Pins, relaxed over coffee as they ordered their food from an extensive menu of prepared meats, grilled hotcakes, assorted Danish pastries and fresh fruits. Goodbody looked at McQuesten and asked,

"Are you anxious to get back to the States?"

"Not really. I know that I'm going to miss seeing you everyday," answered McQuesten as he realized this was the most sincere statement he had made to a woman in years.

Goodbody blushed and answered,

"I know. I'm going to miss you too. After I'm settled at what I'm going to do, perhaps I could come and see you in Washington. You could be my personal guide around the capital of the world. That's how I've heard Washington, DC described."

"That would be fun. Anytime you're ready to travel again, please come and see me," said McQuesten as he wondered what she would think of his abode in McLean, Virginia. Silence prevailed for a few moments.

Goodbody smiled and returned to reading the morning paper gossip column. McQuesten glanced at other people in the dining room. No one set off any alarm bells as he sipped his second coup of coffee. After they had finished breakfast, McQuesten asked Goodbody,

"Do you think it will be strange going back to your apartment after all you've been through?"

"Maybe, I'm not sure. I've thought about it, though. Would you mind terribly walking me up to my apartment? I just don't know what to expect. I'm nervous but I don't know why," said Goodbody as they walked out of the dining room.

"Sure, I understand. It's not a problem. I want to go with you and make sure you're able to settle down after all the trauma I've put you through."

After a quick stop in the restrooms, they walked out the front door and signaled for a taxi. The air was fresh, cool and invigorating. McQuesten did a normal visual check around the door looking for suspicious characters that might set off his senses to danger. No one bothered him.

When they arrived at Goodbody's apartment building, she caught her breath. McQuesten felt her choking up, looked at her and asked,

"Are you all right?"

"Yes, I'm just a little nervous. I guess I'm afraid that you will be saying goodbye soon. It's just a funny feeling."

"Come on, let's get this over with. You'll feel better in no time. I'll stay with you as long as you want me too," said McQuesten as they climbed the steps of her apartment building to the front door.

*   *   *

"Look, there they are, getting out of the taxi," said Murat.

"Yes, the woman and her CIA bodyguard. It makes no difference. We can take care of them after they leave the building," said Francois.

"Yes, it is good that they showed up. I was getting tired of sitting in this car. Maybe now we can take care of business and go home."

The two Frenchmen sat in the Volvo and stared at the front door of Goodbody's apartment building. Finally, Murat said,

"Let's get out of this car and walk down to the corner to get some fresh air and stretch our legs. I want us to be ready when we make a move against these trouble makers."

"Yes, sir. That is a good idea," said Francois.

*   *   *

"Oh, my God," said Goodbody as she walked through the door into her apartment.

"Someone has deliberately trashed everything. This isn't a common burglary. Someone is sending a message that you have to pay for going to Interpol," said McQuesten.

Goodbody couldn't speak. She was so upset seeing her things ruined and smashed into little bits and pieces. She burst into tears.

"We have got to leave. You could be in danger. The people who did this could have your apartment staked-out and be waiting for you. You may be on someone's hit list. It was good that I came back here with you," said McQuesten as he pulled his Beretta out, checked its action and walked to the window to look outside for any suspicious people.

"Is there a backdoor that we can use to leave this building?" asked McQuesten as he saw Goodbody pulling herself together.

"Yes, but it leads into a long narrow dark alley," answered Goodbody.

McQuesten could tell she didn't want to be caught in the alley and she was probably correct. A better idea would be to leave by the front door and grab the first taxi available.

"Okay, let's go back through the front door. As he looked around McQuesten saw the burglars had ripped the telephone line out of the wall.

"Where will we go? Back to the Plaza?" asked Goodbody.

"No, that's too obvious. We need to get moving though. I don't like staying here. The bad-guys could be on their way here right now," said McQuesten as he put his arm around Goodbody's shoulder.

"Okay, let's leave. There is nothing I can do here for now," said Goodbody.

*   *   *

Murat and Francois walked to the corner, which was a short distance from their parked car. Murat thought his two targets had taken too much time to appear. He looked at Francois and said,

"Let's head over to the front door. Perhaps we can catch them unaware and take care of our business in the building."

"Excellent idea, sir," said Francois, who always agreed with the boss.

As the walked up the steps, two little old ladies with their dogs were going through the door for a morning walk. Francois held the door open for them and they thanked him for being so helpful. Little did they know that the two men assisting them were on their way to murder a neighbor.

"This is working out better than I dared to hope," said Murat.

The Frenchmen walked to the elevators and pushed a button to take them up to Goodbody's apartment. The elevators were the European type with open compartments so the occupants could easily see others coming and going to their floors. As Murat and Francois went up, Goodbody and McQuesten were coming down from her floor in the other elevator. As the two elevators passed, Francois tugged at Murat's arm and nodded toward the other elevator going down. McQuesten was innocently watching the other elevator and immediately got bad vibes when he saw the men staring at him.

When Goodbody and McQuesten reach the ground floor, McQuesten grabbed Goodbody's arm and asked,

"Is there a door to the basement near by?"

"Yes, right over there," she answered as she looked around cautiously, and then asked, "What's wrong?"

"Did you happen to notice those men in the other elevator? I think they may be the guys who trashed your apartment," said McQuesten.

Goodbody's hand squeezed McQuesten's arm. She wasn't going to let this man get away from her. McQuesten reached for the door handle and pulled. A single light was burning over the top of the stairs that led down to the basement. The light at the basement landing was burnt out.

Goodbody hesitated initially but then followed McQuesten down the old stairs. The basement was clean but had a musty odor typical of old buildings. He didn't like the looks of it, but there was no choice at this point. There was no light switch visible to get the basement lighted. McQuesten thought perhaps this was good. If these two men followed them down here at least they could hide for a few moments before any trouble started. This dark basement was a better option for them than getting involved in a shoot-out with two men in the hallway.

Goodbody and McQuesten stood in the basement looking for cover. McQuesten saw a stack of large steamer trunks and suitcases the apartment dwellers had placed in storage along the wall. He pulled a golf club from a bag of clubs and handed it to Goodbody, saying,

"Here, take this and don't be afraid to conk one of these guys. I think we are in trouble if they come down here. I'm sure they saw us go through the door. Go over there behind those trunks and stay down low. I'll be over here to cover you and have a better shot at them if they pull their weapons."

Goodbody looked at the golf club and glanced back at McQuesten with a look of resignation as she crouched behind the steamer trunks and suitcases. They heard the door at the top of the steps open. There was no rush of feet coming down the stairway. McQuesten put his index finger to his lips and motioned Goodbody toward the stack of trunks and suitcases.

Francois and Murat slowly moved down the steps of the basement stairway with their guns drawn. Before opening the door to the basement, the two men agreed to shoot their prey on sight. As Francois reached the basement floor he peered into the basement, squinting to focus his eyes in the darkness.

McQuesten held his Beretta ready to fire on either of the men if they made a move against him or Goodbody. After several moments of doing his orientation to the basement darkness, Francois aimed his Walther 9.00 mm automatic and fired one shot at a rack of coats and suits which had created a shadow that he mistook for Goodbody.

McQuesten fired his Beretta from close range and couldn't miss hitting Francois who doubled up in pain from the bullet passing through his torso. He wasn't dead, but it was certainly doubtful how long he'd survive.

Murat saw the flash from the Beretta, aimed his Luger, and fired three rounds where the flash of the gun shot had come from. After pulling the trigger, McQuesten had wisely dropped to the floor and rolled away from his initial position. He heard the slugs fly by and smash into the cement wall behind him. He didn't want to expose his new position but now worried about what Goodbody could do to avoid being hit by the ricocheting bullets.

McQuesten heard feet moving around the floor, but couldn't tell if they were coming toward him or going away. No one made any noise for about fifteen seconds. A trunk, or suitcase, fell from atop a pile and crashed to the floor. This was an old trick to distract a person and get them to give up their position by shooting at the noise.

McQuesten didn't move but waited for another noise. The next moment he heard someone yelling in pain. It was a man's deep voice. Then he heard the golf club he had given Goodbody fall to the floor. McQuesten ventured a small peek around a stack of trunks and saw a man rubbing his shin bone with one hand. The other hand was pointing a Luger toward a pile of boxes and suitcases. The man squeezed off two shots into the boxes. Goodbody screamed. McQuesten leveled his Beretta and fired two shots at the man who held the Luger. The gun dropped to the floor and the man slumped over dead.

McQuesten yelled,

"Sophie, are you all right?"

"Yes, but I'm very frightened. What's happening?" Goodbody's voice was trembling.

"Don't move. Stay right where you are. I'll check these guys to make sure they're dead."

McQuesten slowly moved away from his pile of suit-cases and steamer trunks. He found the first man dead at the stairwell landing. The second man was also dead from two shots hitting him squarely in the chest. His Luger pistol was lying next to his dead body. McQuesten pushed at the man's body with his foot and confirmed that he wasn't playing possum.

"Okay, it's safe to come out."

Goodbody rose from behind some boxes and said, "I'm not injured, but will this never end?" She walked to McQuesten and began to shake and cry tears of relief.

"I can't imagine who will come after you now. We've killed a lot of bad-guys over this money laundering business. Come on, let's go upstairs and call the police. We've got to plug-in Ramsey and the American Embassy. He can help to clear up any questions the police will have," said McQuesten.

When Goodbody and McQuesten reached the main floor several ladies who lived in the building were standing near the basement door wondering about the gun shots.

McQuesten looked at a woman and said,

"There are two dead men in the basement. They tried to kill Miss Goodbody. There was a gun battle and I shot them. Please call the police and ask them to come here immediately."

The startled woman, with wide eyes, looked at McQuesten and said, "Yes, sir, right away." She disappeared into her apartment and ran to her telephone.

A shaken Goodbody, leaning on McQuesten, said,

"I want to call my mother. I need to hear her voice and let her know I'm back in Copenhagen. Perhaps I should stay with her tonight."

McQuesten thought to himself that Goodbody was making a good decision to leave Copenhagen and spend time with her mother. Then a thought came to him.

"It will be good for you to go to your mother's house, but give me her telephone number, please."

The Juan les-Pins Affair

10

Vladimir Zhukov was born in Moscow, the only child of parents well-connected politically within the Communist Party. His father was able to arrange his education at the best private schools in Moscow. For elective subjects, he chose English and French. The parents of his fellow students were diplomats and high ranking military officers. Athletically, he excelled at soccer and swimming. He was a strong swimmer and was able to hold his breath underwater longer than any of his classmates.

Upon graduation from Moscow University he was employed as a trainee at the state controlled oil and gas ministry. He began his career as an oil analyst and rose quickly through the ranks of the bureaucracy. These duties enabled him to develop strong relationships with executives of western European oil and gas companies. As he grew older his appearance took on a portly look of an executive who was destined for command. His hair line was receding slightly and he was becoming gray around the temples.

When the Cold War ended, Russia shifted high grade steel manufacturing from military equipment to oil drilling bits, routers and pipeline construction materials. Exploration and development of Russia's vast Siberian oil and gas reserves became a top priority within the state planning commissions.

As Zhukov rose in the bureaucracy of the state Oil and Gas Ministry, he learned about backroom deals, bribes and other fraud that characterized the industry. Although he did not pursue bribes personally, many western oil companies were ready to hand out generous cash payments to obtain the secret results of the aggressive Russian exploration test wells, projected pipeline routes and Siberian oil leases that were becoming available. Small villages east of the Ural Mountains like Surgut, Tyumen and Nizhnevartovsk became Siberian oil boom towns because they were sitting on huge fields of oil and gas reserves. Western European oil companies were prepared to offer any amounts of cash to get the rights to become development partners with Russia and its reserves.

During a state-sponsored trip to France, Zhukov met a woman in Marseilles employed by the French oil importing authority. During his business trips outside of Russia Zhukov met many women but he considered this lady special. As he traveled more widely in Europe he became aware of the Russian organized crime syndicates and his potential for making a personal fortune. Zhukov began to give serious thought to leaving Russian and living in Western Europe.

During another trip to Marseilles, he attended a dinner party with other European oil executives. As the dinner party was breaking up, Zhukov was approached by several Russians who said they represented a French oil consortium. Because of his invaluable knowledge of the Russian oil fields they offered him a lucrative position in Marseilles. After listening to their offer and investigating the men further, Zhukov learned that they were members of a crime syndicate that controlled racketeering interests connected to the importation of crude oil along the Cote d' Azur.

In the early years of the Russian privatization of its oil industry, one large oil company, Yukos, began its rise to preeminence. Zhukov's work with the Yukos exploration teams gave him special insight into their oil and gas lease holdings. Zhukov was considered a blue-chip acquisition for an organization that wanted to do business in Russia. With the huge amounts of money being offered, Zhukov decided to leave the Russian oil ministry, move to Marseilles, marry the French woman and join the Russian organized crime family. Their specialty was bribery and pay-offs within the European oil markets. It did not take long for Zhukov to rise to the top in his new crime family. Life was now good for Zhukov.

While working at the Oil Ministry, he became close to many Iraqi oil & gas managers. He visited Baghdad several times to finalize agreements and establish business deals for Iraqi oil to flow into southern Russia. Zhukov signed deals for Petroval, an oil shipping subsidiary and the natural gas giant Gazrom. As a result of this work, he had extensive knowledge of the key managers within the Iraqi oil industry.

When the UN sanctions were put in place against Iraq, Saddam Hussein and the Iraqi people were caught in an economic squeeze. To relieve this hardship, the UN began its Oil for Food Program, ostensibly to help the suffering people of Iraq. This UN program set the stage for Zhukov's crime family to engage in fraud and to offer financial kick-backs to Saddam Hussein.

Shortly after Zhukov joined the crime syndicate, two of their senior men were killed in an automobile crash while attending a meeting in Paris. No foul play was proven, but in their business it was natural to be suspicious of accidents that happened to your top people. Because of his oil background, Zhukov was promoted rapidly to a key management position in the Russian crime syndicate. He moved the headquarters of the crime syndicate to a downtown office building which they had acquired in settlement of a debt owed by one of their victims. The building security was upgraded across the board. The other firms leasing space in the building were forced out. Professional security guards were hired to monitor the building security 24/7. Communication and computer services were installed that offered the newest technology available. Zhukov's private office was large and spacious. It was decorated with expensive saddle-colored leather – full grain, aniline-dyed sofas plus massive leather chairs placed throughout. A dark walnut paneled specially-designed entertainment wet bar was installed in his office. It was stocked with the very best French wines and Russian vodka. Old expensive oriental rugs covered the floor of his office. Modern art prints were carefully hung on all available wall space. Living well was the best revenge, Zhukov often said to himself.

Zhukov adopted several corporate names for his crime syndicate, which enabled them to do business posing as a legitimate oil consortium. This also made his activity of money laundering easier with the French, Italian and off-shore banking networks that were used to support his activities. His shell companies inconspicuously carried names such as Green Corporation, Russian French Oil Trading Corporation and Maximov Oil Trading, LLC. These were hardly household names, but they wouldn't raise the eyebrows of law enforcement agencies.

As Zhukov expanded his crime syndicate, fellow Russian businessmen in Cyprus began offering him deals that were difficult to pass up. Smuggling oil was easy because Zhukov knew that business, but now he had opportunities to make money in diamond smuggling, weapons, lumber and drugs from central Asia. He stopped short and drew the line at the white slave trade. He recruited former associates from Moscow and brought them into his management group in Marseilles. Any challenges or attacks by competitors were met with a ruthless reaction typical of every Russian crime organization.

*   *   *

"Vladimir, Yuri here. I need to speak with you about a diamond deal. Very secret and highly profitable for both of us; when can we talk?"

"What are you saying, Yuri? You know I am in the oil business, not diamonds."

"Vladimir, I have my top men involved in this deal. These diamonds are rough-cut stones; the best quality stones from South Africa, being sold secretly by Muslims to raise cash."

"Interesting," said Zhukov.

"I need your Antwerp contacts to move this merchandise quietly; also with no questions being asked. I'm offering you twenty per cent. Our seller is anxious to deal. When can we meet?" asked Yuri.

Zhukov listened to Yuri's voice as well as his words. He had learned long ago not to appear too anxious when negotiating with another Russian.

"I'll have to think about this for a day or so. How much are we talking about?"

Yuri was waiting for this question. Now he knew Zhukov was seriously interested. Yuri cleared his throat and lowered his voice, paused, and said,

"The stones are worth five million – American. Your cut will be one million if we can deal immediately. My Muslim friends are nervous."

Zhukov had previously concluded several small precious stone deals, so he knew where to sell the diamonds. Russians had been selling industrial diamonds in Antwerp for years. These markets were controlled by DeBeers and Lev Levier, a Russian Jew in Israel.

Zhukov had heard rumors that diamonds were being sold by terrorists to purchase weapons. In the trade they were referred to as "Blood Diamonds." Because the United States government had squeezed and pressured the al-Qaeda money channels, plus freezing Arab bank accounts, the terrorist's money was being invested in the world diamond markets. Diamonds were easy to ship around the world and held their value better than currency. Zhukov had no problem accepting diamonds in lieu of currency to arrange a weapons deal with a front company for a terrorist group. The next morning Zhukov called his Cyprus connection.

"Yuri, I'm curious what your Muslim client will do with the money he receives from the sale of the diamonds?"

"Weapons; AK-47s, ammunition, RPGs and SA-8 missiles; my client has a large weapons order. These rough cut diamonds are just the down-payment. Are you interested in his supplying weapons to these people? I'm sure I can set up a deal for you with them."

"Yes. I want to participate in both sides of this deal. What about an end-user certificate? That could complicate things for me," said Zhukov.

"Not necessary. Don't worry about it."

"If I get the order for the weapons you can bring me the stones tomorrow," said Zhukov as he waited for his answer.

"That could be a problem."

"I know you can work it out. I'll wait to hear from you. Do zvidaniya"

Zhukov looked over his notes and filed them in his daily journal. Zhukov knew that by placing pressure on Yuri he would in turn squeeze his Muslim client and get the weapons order. Zhukov didn't like any extra paper-work. Paper-trail problems never come-up if there's no paper-work, thought Zhukov. The telephone on his large desk rang.

"Yes."

"Something has happened with the Iraqi National Bank in Cannes," said Zhukov's second in command.

"Tell me what you have heard."

"Rumor has it that Interpol and the American CIA have siphoned all the money from Saddam's bank with special routing numbers obtained from a bank in Copenhagen."

"Did we get hurt?" asked Zhukov.

"Only our business pipeline was destroyed. No funds were lost by us, but our business arrangements with Baghdad are finished."

"Someone must pay a heavy penalty for this attack. Can Murat handle this job? It's his area of the Cote d'Azur," said Zhukov.

"Yes, I will set it up if you approve." Zhukov thought for a few moments to make sure that he wasn't moving too quickly. Then he responded,

"Set it up, but make sure we have complete deniability."

"No problem," said Zhukov's number two man.

"Keep me informed," said Zhukov as he replaced the telephone receiver in its cradle. It was early but he walked to his bar and poured a drink. Zhukov reflected a moment; if Interpol could bring down the Iraqi bank, what could keep them from attacking his BNP Paribas bank accounts? Zhukov lit a small Turkish cigar and sipped his drink. These were the things that kept him awake at night. Zhukov reminded himself to review his banking relationship in Geneva the next morning.

*   *   *

After Donald Winkler Nelson was nominated to the post of Assistant Director of Central Intelligence for Analysis and Production, he was approved by the Senate without any of the rancor other nominees had received in the past. Upon assuming his duties, Nelson committed himself to strengthening the intelligence gathering capability of the Middle Eastern field offices. Nelson told the headquarters staff that it was imperative to select and promote younger officers who could aggressively build up agent networks in Cairo, Istanbul and Beirut. This effort would be critical for success in any protracted struggle with the Muslim world. He realized it wouldn't be easy for his station chiefs to recruit Muslim agents. Large cash payments were available for recruitment, but the field offices discovered money didn't motivate Muslims. The files were full of intelligence American diplomats picked up in Tel Aviv. Nelson refused to be dependent on intelligence passed along by Meir Dagan and the Mossad.

Begrudgingly, Congress had expanded his budget to allow hiring of Semitic and Ural-Altaic linguists to work at headquarters, analyzing the raw intelligence from the Middle East. Money was tight, so budget constraints were the mode. Many Senators said that spy satellites could provide all the intelligence that was necessary.

It was his sense that Senators on the Appropriations Committee had little enthusiasm about expanding his budget. After serving five years as the Assistant DCI he knew his tenure was dependent upon the pleasure of the President. Press murmurs that he was "long in the tooth" appeared constantly. Also, his wife cautioned him to avoid sounding like a "has-been." These comments were hard to accept. He vowed to use his remaining time as a ball of fire.

Nelson's desk was piled with files marked, "Secret-Eyes Only." Iron Hand's money-laundering covert action file occupied his attention daily. This mission was now moving fast. He was anxious to read the progress reports. So far, no one in the press corps or TV media had picked-up on this European operation. Nelson thought, "Maybe we'll get Iron Hand through his mission without a media leak." While musing about leaks, his mind jumped to the often- heard rumor of a mole in the CIA. "Could this be possible," he wondered? "My God, perish the thought." There had been no news of any blown agent networks or compromised actions. He dismissed his concerns of a CIA mole, as he placed Iron Hand's file to the side. Leaks to the media were his concern. "Where were these damn media leaks coming from," he wondered?

*   *   *

"DCI on your number two line," said Tilghman's secretary and chief protector. He stretched for the phone.

"Yes sir, what can I do for you?"

"I haven't heard much about Iron Hand and his latest assignment. What's going on with him? Do you know anything new? Come over and talk to me. I've got a few other items we need to kick around."

"Yes sir, I'll be right there."

Tilghman grabbed his Iron Hand file and headed out the door and down the hall. As Deputy DCI, Tilghman had massive intelligence responsibilities that included covert actions and the INTEL analytical unit responsible for evaluations done by a staff of two dozen women who worked around the clock. Tilghman thought to himself, if Iron Hand stuck to his schedule he'd be stateside in three, maybe four days.

"You're comfortable with Iron Hand's progress in Europe with this money laundering action?" asked the DCI as he eased back in his chair behind his desk.

"Yes. I don't anticipate any problems. I haven't had a report from Iron Hand in two days but that's par for the course on this kind of operation," said Tilghman.

"Okay, let's switch to another subject unless you've got something else."

"No, nothing further, sir," said Tilghman.

The DCI picked up a file on his desk, opened it up and read some notes. He looked up at Tilghman.

"My sources in the Senate have told me that several Senators are going to attempt to embarrass me and the CIA when I testify in a hearing scheduled for next week up on the Hill. I need some good comments to throw back at them after I am finished with my opening remarks. Do you have any ideas?"

"Yes sir, for openers I'd like to say I have a lot of ideas about fighting terrorism and not fighting ourselves. We have our best people brain-storming every imaginable scenario with detailed responses to a multitude of contingencies. For example, when Nixon invaded Cambodia to destroy the Viet Cong sanctuary the Left went totally berserk. Now when we didn't arbitrarily cross into Pakistan to hunt down Usama bin Laden the same Left is critical because we're not being aggressive. You'd think these politicians were on the other side, the way they talk in front of a microphone and camera. Where were these people when the page was blank? Where were these Senators when we asked for money to build our capacity with more agents in the Middle East? They were no where to be found," said Tilghman.

"Yes, these are good points, but I can't say those words in open testimony. I need something that says the same thing but it must be more subtle," said the DCI.

"May I have a day or so to polish up these points? Perhaps we could meet later and discuss some refined ideas?" asked Tilghman.

"Good, go to work on that. I'll be interested in what you come up with."

*   *   *

After this meeting with the DCI, Tilghman returned to his office to reflect on developing talking points for the DCI at his Senate testimony. Tilghman closed the door for some privacy and sat down in his chair. He closed his eyes, propped his feet on the corner of his desk, and let his mind roll back to his school days, searching for some perspective. For some reason, he remembered a story his father had told him about his grade school baseball coach telephoning his father to discuss his son's playing.

"Mr. Tilghman, this is Bob Elliott. I am the baseball coach at George's school. If you have a few minutes, I'd like to talk to you about George."

"Mr. Elliott, thank you for calling. What's on your mind?"

"Mr. Tilghman, George tried real hard this season and he played well when we could get him into the games. However, I don't think he is cut out to be a baseball player. I think he'd do better at swimming or maybe running cross-country. He'd feel better about himself and probably build up his body more than shagging flies in the outfield. I thought you should know this rather than have George get down on himself about not being as good as some of his team mates. I hope I haven't disappointed you by mentioning these things about your son."

"No, not at all. I feel the same way and I'm happy you called. I'll talk to George tonight and leave you out of it. It was very nice of you to take the time to call me."

Tilghman remembered that later that evening his dad had asked him to sit down next to him on their front porch.

"George, let's talk about some area of athletics where you might be able to excel, maybe even become really good," said George's father.

"You know Dad, I've been thinking about this too. I don't think I'm cut out for baseball, football or basketball. Maybe track or swimming would be best for me?" George said to his father.

The next day George was back to his old self, feeling good that he wouldn't have to compete on the fields with guys he didn't feel he matched up with physically. It was a new day and he was now on the right path, thanks to his father's good intuition.

*   *   *

Tilghman locked his school boy memories into a corner of his mind. He then began recalling the CIA covert action folklore from the Eisenhower administration that yielded relative easy successes in Iran, Guatemala and the Philippines.

In the early days of the Kennedy administration the failure at the Bay of Pigs gave liberal politicians who were uneasy with the CIA an opportunity to glance in their rearview mirror and find perfect clarity. President Kennedy raised the consciousness by recalling a famous saying, "Victory has a hundred fathers and defeat is an orphan."

Perhaps 1975 was the worst period for the CIA, during which time a Congressional investigation by the Senate Select Committee head, the grand-standing Idaho Senator Frank Church, demanded answers to questions of national security in open public testimony.

The DCI has the consistent goal to provide the President and his administration with objective truth, so the President can formulate his policy and action plans. On many occasions the objective truth provided by the DCI isn't what the Presidential security advisors want to hear.

The CIA has learned through bitter experience that if any covert action is to be successful, three basic elements must be in place; a determined will to succeed, a willingness to take domestic political risks if the CA causes public disclosures and, finally, the will and ability to provide military support.

CIA field officers consider themselves front-line 24/7 activists doing business in the trenches. Furthermore, field officers view the headquarters staff as expert second-guessing bureaucrats who work forty hours a week. The Langley staffers view the field officers as living high on the hog with overseas cost of living adjustments who do not handle agents efficiently.

Tilghman had seen two Presidents come and go but this President from the southwest wasn't like his predecessors. He embraced the concept of CA but at the same time saw its limitations. Signal intelligence was coming on strong at the NSA and was in many ways more reliable than field officers and agents combing the backwoods for intelligence about an enemy's intentions. The President recognized that a big part of the CIA capability was covert action, plus it was a real morale booster when a CA mission was successful.

Tilghman was confident that he could predict verbatim what the National Security Council would say about any question concerning approval of a CA against an aggressor country. The State Department would counsel going slow, recommend containment and then negotiations. State would then express concern over the world reaction and the image of the USA at the UN. The Defense Department would push for direct action or saber rattling along the borders and increased listening by NRO surveillance satellites.

Aside from this, it was now slowly dawning in the minds of the upper-echelon administration officials that massive military action wasn't the smartest way to wage war against terrorism. Smaller CA missions against carefully chosen targets were just as effective and the terrorists always knew who was hitting them. A strong CA against a terrorist group could solve problems for years, if not forever.

During his last meeting in the White House the President said that he wanted to take actions that would make a difference, not just playing tit-for-tat. The President wasn't committed to a policy of regime changes but the status quo and containment scenarios used by his predecessors had proven ineffective. The days of tin-horn dictators playing off the USSR against the USA were over. With the Soviet Union out of the equation, different pressures could be brought to bear against small nations that supported terrorism, drug smuggling, money laundering, arms sales and organized crime syndicates. This made it imperative to develop contingency plans on the shelf and keep them ready until the right opportunity presented itself. When all the balls were lined up perfectly and the right CA plan was available, the President could quickly "run the table" against a despotic dictator and the world would be happily rid of an international despot.

Tilghman grew up in the Boston area and graduated from Brown University, majoring in pre-medicine. He was granted a deferred acceptance at Johns Hopkins Medical School until he completed his military service. Upon receiving his commission from OCS, he served as an Admiral's aide for three years in Europe at NATO headquarters. Becoming spoiled working at NATO headquarters for three years, he felt that six years of sea duty wasn't appealing. His other choice was returning to medical school, living like a monk, and hitting the books for four years. The Navy beckoned and Tilghman accepted an offer to join the regular Navy.

Tilghman pulled three years of sea duty in the Atlantic on a cargo ship and then received orders to the Sixth Fleet in Naples, Italy as an assistant operations officer. His wife joined him and for three years they lived the good life in an apartment fit for a king. His next duty was back to BuPers in Washington, DC, where he was noticed by his old boss, Admiral Rogers, now a three-stripe flag officer in the CIA. Admiral Rogers was functioning as the Chief Human Resources Officer. Later Rogers called Tilghman and said,

"We have plenty of Commanders who can drive ships. We need officers at headquarters who can plan and think outside of the box. Go buy a house in Virginia and get used to working at Langley."

As they say, the rest is history.

The Juan les-Pins Affair

11

The American Embassy in Copenhagen was situated on a quiet downtown corner at the intersection of tree lined streets that presented a park-like atmosphere. McQuesten and Ramsey relaxed in a third-floor private meeting room, slowly sipping strong black coffee. McQuesten thought to himself, "Danes brew excellent morning coffee." It was nine A.M. as they reviewed their report which summarized what had gone down with the Iraqi bank money laundering case, concluding with the attempted assassination of Goodbody by two Juan les-Pins gangsters.

"So now what happens? Where do we go from here?" asked Ramsey; he seemed perplexed about the future life of their covert action mission. The two CIA officers were not ready to bring down the curtain on their mission but they needed authority from headquarters to continue the operation.

"Well, obviously there is more on our plate now than just a case of stopping dirty money moving around the European banking system," said McQuesten.

"For openers, there was a leak somewhere on our side to the Russian crime family concerning Goodbody's role in providing the Iraqi bank routing numbers," said McQuesten as he drained his coffee cup and pushed it aside. McQuesten's face registered a frown and it was easy to see he was puzzled how a leak could be passed to the Russian crime syndicate. He sensed that the leak could have been inadvertent. But, it may have also been clandestine. He wondered what they were dealing with inside of Interpol.

"Yes, I agree. We have to investigate where the lapse of security occurred and who passed this information along to the crime operators in Juan les-Pins. That job must be a top priority," said Ramsey.

"Did Interpol identify the two men who tried to kill us in the apartment building?" asked McQuesten.

"Yes. It took some doing, but they got the job done," answered Ramsey as he pushed the Interpol file along the desk to Iron Hand.

"Those two hit-men had direct ties to a Russian mob in Marseilles. We didn't find ID in their pockets, but we got positive results from their finger prints and mug shots in the Interpol data bank."

"Do we go back into the lion's den and try to knock out this Russian crime family? What are the odds that we get cleared to go after the Russians since they sent killers to eliminate us?" McQuesten mused to himself.

"It just depends how deeply headquarters is going to let us dig, but I'll wager 50-50 that Langley will give us the green light," said Ramsey as he shrugged and pumped his fist.

"You know, I like enthusiasm, but I hope you're not proposing a deal like, "Why don't you and he go fight,' " said McQuesten with a frown and a smirk.

"No, no. I'll be with you all the way if we get the approval to go after these Russians in Marseilles."

"Plus your friends from Interpol, they'll be able to help too?" McQuesten inquired, looking for support.

"Sure, Interpol will cooperate fully. We also need to get support from the French counter-espionage service. We will have to be careful about tipping our hand but we will need the DST people if we tackle the Russians in Marseilles. All these law enforcement agencies would love to knock off an active Russian crime operation. My guess is these Russians wheel and deal in all the crime activities in Western Europe: weapons, diamonds, dope, money laundering and smuggling old WW II art treasures. We are overdue for the good guys to nail one of these Russian crime syndicates."

"Speaking again of Interpol, they processed all the banking data from Goodbody's secret routing numbers. The leak could have come from someone working in their banking units," said McQuesten, as he made a mental note about giving Interpol too much information about his plans.

"Yeah, I was thinking about that too. Kind of hard to believe, but it's possible," said Ramsey, as he retrieved the case file and looked through it again.

"I'll have to wait on headquarters, but I'm all for it, since we've come this far. Besides, I don't like knowing that an international crime boss will be plotting to get even with me somewhere down the line. I'd like to take him out now," said McQuesten as he tried to picture Tilghman and his staff reviewing his request to go after the Russians.

"Good. Let me know what headquarters says," said Ramsey, as he closed the file and put it in his briefcase.

"I don't think we'll have to wait too long. These people at headquarters can move fast."

*   *   *

"What do we have in our files about the Russian mobsters in Marseilles?" asked Tilghman of the six women INTEL analysts sitting at his office conference-room table. Inside his file he had a top priority message request from Iron Hand to extend his stay in Europe and work with Ramsey, plus the French DST and Interpol, to do battle with the Russian crime syndicate. Tilghman promised Iron Hand an answer in twenty-four hours. Iron Hand had signaled that he felt highly confident they could take down the Russian mobsters. Tilghman knew that the DCI was concerned that the covert action plan was starting to look for more trouble than they had originally planned to handle. DCI wasn't anxious to get Iron Hand and Ramsey in over their heads. Before he signaled a green light to Iron Hand, he wanted to be satisfied any action had a high probability of success.

"We know where they operate, what they do and most of their top people," said the INTEL section leader as she paused, glanced around the table and then continued,

"They are involved in all the usual crime activity: drugs, lumber, diamond smuggling, weapons traffic of various descriptions and money laundering throughout Western Europe. Their specialty of late has been the OFFP kick-backs to Saddam Hussein. They have established several front companies to handle the Iraqi crude oil business with Saddam's shell corporations."

Tilghman listened to their opening statements and let the information sink into his memory banks before asking,

"What are their weaknesses? Where do we think we can successfully attack their organization?"

The INTEL section leader shuffled a few papers to let everyone know she was ready for this question. She looked directly at Tilghman and began her analysis.

"Business has been so good for these criminals it's quite possible they may be getting sloppy. They probably have stretched themselves thin and have been guilty of accepting too many deals on blind faith from their business partners. However, it's no secret that if these Russians in Marseilles get hammered or double-crossed in a deal, they move aggressively to eliminate anyone they think cheated them. Nothing really new about that kind of reaction, if they get ripped-off and are stuck holding the bag, so to speak," said the section leader.

"Okay, what are your ideas?" asked Tilghman, who added, "I'm dealing with a short time frame here, if we are going to authorize action against this Russian syndicate."

"Our consensus is that the best method to attack these Russians is via their oil tanker smuggling operation. This relates directly to the OFFP the UN is supervising. It's the easiest way for us to get close to them and follow their paper trail which will include banking and oil commodity trading accounts. We could nail them on wire-fraud plus conspiracy to commit fraud, smuggling oil into France without proper tanker cargo documentation. There would be a record of pay-offs to dock and port authorities. Their pay-off schemes may even go higher to French governmental officials. We might get a few people to confess and then use their testimony as

State witnesses to nail some big fish in the crime syndicate," said the section leader.

"I like these ideas. There has been some good home-work done here," said Tilghman as he glanced around the table and saw a few smiles.

"Our contacts at Interpol have been shadowing a tanker named the Basra Queen. The Captain and First Officer have been actively running small-time smuggling of drugs, expensive cars, and weapons. In addition, our informants have told us that the Iraqi oil ministry may be involved in a racket known as oil topping-off with this Captain and the Basra Queen. We have the goods on Captain Ghadi and the First Officer. Interpol feels confident they can get these two men to cooperate with the authorities to nail the Russian crime bosses," said the INTEL section leader.

Tilghman listened and agreed with the assessment of his INTEL staff. He looked around the table and could tell they wanted to hear his decision.

"Okay, I've heard enough. I'll approve McQuesten's request for further action against the Russian mobsters in Marseilles. Flash our approval and give him what ever he needs to get the job done."

When the meeting broke up, the INTEL staff people felt good about their role in taking action against the crime syndicate in Europe. Departmental morale jumped a few notches as the women staffers walked back to their desks.

*   *   *

Ramsey and McQuesten flew back to Nice, France, traveling in the same chartered Lear jet that they used to extract themselves from their earlier troubles on the Cote d' Azur. The two men checked into McQuesten's favorite beach-side hotel, La Villa Juanaise. They were finishing up a late lunch when Ramsey began to outline his tentative plan.

"Here's our plan of action: disguised as insurance company representatives we will joined the Basra Queen tanker in Cyprus and ride with them to Marseilles. Interpol has arranged all our fake ID and letters of introduction to the Captain. The Captain shouldn't be alarmed that two Yanks are riding on his tanker, because the ship has been refinanced through a consortium of American banks. We will hang out in the officer's mess and living compartments for the six day run to Marseilles. Our main focus will be to keep our eyes and ears open for any incriminating evidence that leads to our target, the Russian crime syndicate.

"Sounds good. I haven't been to sea for some time. I like the idea of breathing some salty air," said McQuesten.

"I thought you'd like this arrangement," said Ramsey as he finished a second glass of ice tea.

"How do we get to Cyprus?"

Ramsey pulled out two Air France first-class tickets and flashed them at McQuesten.

"We leave tomorrow morning at 0930 for Cyprus from the Nice airport. By flying commercial I think we draw less attention to ourselves."

"Good thinking."

The two men separated as Ramsey headed to his hotel room. McQuesten decided to walk along the street sidewalks to relax, soaking up the downtown atmosphere inspecting the store windows that catered to tourists. After walking several blocks McQuesten came to a park lined with palm trees that was used by old retired Frenchmen to play boules ball. These were serious players of boules. There were many Frenchmen watching every move the players made. Suddenly McQuesten thought there could be a spy in the park watching his movements. He left and walked a new route back to his hotel.

*   *   *

Zhukov was seated behind his massive, expensive French mahogany desk in his office building, reviewing his notes from recent telephone conversations with his men. He had been upset for the last week over the loss in Copenhagen of his top man Jacques Murat, and his number two man. The phone rang on his desk. Zhukov reached for the receiver,

"Yes."

"I've checked around Copenhagen and I've been able to piece together what happened to Murat and Francois," said Zhukov's office assistant.

"Good, tell me what you have learned."

"Murat and Francois planned to murder the woman from the Copenhagen bank and the CIA officer who was her companion. They trashed the woman's apartment hoping to panic her into running away. Then they planned to kill her in the city. Somehow Murat and Francois got involved in a shoot-out in the basement of the apartment house and were killed. The woman and her CIA companion escaped unharmed. Our spies have learned that Interpol identified our two men and are staking-out Murat's headquarters in Juan les-Pins. Do you want to take any action?" asked Zhukov's assistant.

"No. Right now, we do nothing. We've lost two rounds to these people. I'm willing to take a pass for now. We will wait and see if they make any moves against us here. We can always go back and pick up against them later. Right now we'll sit tight and consolidate our losses. These people are big, tough and well organized. I'm not looking for a direct confrontation against Interpol, the French DST or the CIA."

"Very good sir, I will advise you if I hear any news or rumors in the street that shed more light on what happened. There is one more thing we should talk about."

"Yes, what is that?"

"We have been contacted by a thirty-four year old Russian who grew up in St. Petersburg. He's looking for a position in our organization. He speaks fluent English and some French. He is an ex-Russian army officer who specialized in artillery atomic warheads. He had extensive battle experience in Afghanistan's northern province of Badakhshan. After leaving the Russian army he lived in

London. He worked as an independent contractor with Egyptian Muslims in a terror plot in the States. Their plot was busted by the CIA and FBI. He was arrested, convicted and sentenced to a prison term. He was able to get help from a Russian gang in Brighton Beach, New York. They arranged his escape back to Europe."

"Sounds interesting, what's his name?"

"Sergei Bruslov."

"Arrange a meeting as soon as practical. We can use a man like this. Tell him I'm interested in meeting with him."

"I will handle this right away."

"Yes, let's leave things that way for now, but keep me informed."

Zhukov put down the telephone and looked out the window to think about his situation. Why ask for more trouble with the CIA or Interpol? Murat was stupid to go to Copenhagen and get involved in a gun battle. It would have been wiser to send a trusted member of his organization to get the job done. A leader never goes out on a mission to kill someone. A leader orders others to do his dirty-work. That's why we have these people in our organization. Dumb, really dumb, thought Zhukov. "It's time to think and organize my thoughts. Focus, and then refocus," thought Zhukov. Concentrate on your short-term planning Zhukov said to himself. Zhukov thought to himself, "Perhaps a good stiff drink of vodka would settle me down." He looked over at his bar but didn't give in to this temptation. He thought about the man from St. Petersburg. Maybe he could take over Murat's operation.

*   *   *

When Iron Hand walked through the Nice airport he carefully glanced around the concourse, looking for any suspicious Iraqis who might be involved in surveillance. After his last visit to this airport he wasn't taking anything for granted. His internal warning system was passive, so he relaxed as he walked through the passenger security check point. His Beretta pistol plus several extra clips of bullets were packed away in his checked luggage. What with the state of security in Nice, he didn't expect his bags to be x-rayed. Ramsey had also packed a weapon in his baggage. The two CIA officers were ready for any action that came along. Iron Hand knew that he and Ramsey were going into harm's way. They weren't just dressed up for trouble, they were now looking for it.

"What's our plan after we arrive in Cyprus?" asked Iron Hand, as they walked on the tarmac toward the AirBus two-engine jet.

Ramsey looked behind to make certain there were no convenient listeners who might be attempting to eavesdrop on their conversation. Satisfied everything was cool, he answered McQuesten.

"Real simple; after we clear security, we take a cab directly to the Basra Queen. The tanker has been in Limassol for two days, off-loading about half of its oil cargo. Marseilles is the next port of call for the tanker. Cyprus has turned into a modern-day hang-out for criminals and scam artists dealing with all sorts of Middle East intrigue. The two most active sectors for smuggling involve automatic weapons like AK-47s and RPGs, followed by heroin from the Golden Triangle. The dope goes directly into the organized crime processing labs in Marseilles. By using our insurance representative cover, we can play it straight and low-key during the trip. By keeping our ears open we might pick up some good information that will help us knock off these Russians."

"Is there a chance that we may get some needed co-operation from the Captain and his First Lieutenant?" asked Iron Hand.

"Yes, the First Lieutenant has been told that he is on an Interpol watch list for small time smuggling. The Captain hasn't been approached but these guys are too smart not to cooperate with Interpol. They could have their Masters papers pulled by Interpol and they would be beached for life. They'd wind up being bar tenders along the Cote d' Azur if they're lucky."

"Okay, I'm in your hands," said McQuesten, who was interested in the super tanker and her sea worthiness.

*   *   *

Zhukov sat alone in his office looking over some notes from yesterday's action. The loss of his top man in Juan les-Pins still nagged at him. It was difficult to replace men to run an organization. Perhaps this new Russian from London could be used in the Juan les-Pins organization. Time would tell. Middle management guys and street bosses were easy enough to recruit but he was reluctant to become directly involved. He also needed to talk with his man, Yuri, in Cyprus about their diamond and weapons deal. He picked up his cell phone and punched out the private numbers to Cyprus.

"Where do we stand on our diamonds and weapons deal, Yuri?" asked Zhukov who was anxious to get some solid action going after his losses in Copenhagen and Cannes.

"Last night my Muslim client delivered the diamonds to me. I am reluctant to risk flying the diamonds directly to Marseilles. I know that an oil tanker, the Basra Queen, is leaving Cyprus today for Marseilles. The Captain is reliable and has worked for me before. I am going to consign the diamonds to him for delivery to you in about a week. I think you may know this man. The tanker has been used to smuggle oil into the French port on several occasions. I believe there may be some extra oil on this tanker for delivery in Marseilles. I hope this meets with your approval. On this trip you will get diamonds and oil. Two for one," said Yuri, with a little chuckle in his voice.

"Yes, I know Captain Ghadi. This is a satisfactory arrangement. Yuri, you have done a good job in setting up this transaction. Why can't everyone do business like this? Zhukov asked rhetorically.

"Because they aren't Russians, like you and me."

"You are probably right. Keep me informed about all the details with this transaction. I have lined up the weapons on the Muslims purchase list. There will be no problem providing everything they want." Zhukov was not prepared to end the conversation.

"Good, very, good. I will stay in touch. I have paid the Muslims for their diamonds so you must pay me after you sell them in Antwerp. You can credit my account in Marseilles to keep it simple," said Yuri with a happy note in his voice. Zhukov could tell that Yuri was concerned, having paid the Muslim for the full amount of the diamonds before they were sold, and before Zhukov had taken his commission to handle the sale of the diamonds.

"Don't worry. You will get all your money, Yuri."

Yuri paused and then said, "I know that I can trust you because you are a Russian and a man of your word."

"Yes, you are correct. I am a man of my word."

*   *   *

Iron Hand and Ramsey rode in a taxi from the Cyprus airport onto the pier next to the moored Basra Queen. The tanker looked massive, since she had risen in the water after unloading half of her oil cargo. Iron Hand initially received no bad vibes about going aboard the tanker, as he and Ramsey stood alone on the pier after getting out of the taxi. Iron Hand let his eyes shift from fore to aft and then looked carefully at the superstructure of the tanker.

"Do you see the array of electronic antennae mounted aft of the bridge?" asked Ramsey, as he nodded his head toward the ship. "It looks a little overdone for a tanker; more like the gear the Russian trawlers use to listen in on our fleet communications in the Mediterranean."

"Yes, I see what you mean. I'd say the Captain isn't using that electronic gear to listen to the evening news from the BBC," answered Iron Hand.

"Yeah, but how about eavesdropping on law enforcement traffic or perhaps sending special encrypted communications to some drug czar who's shipping a load of heroin into Marseilles," said Ramsey. They walked up the forward brow gangway and met a well dressed Duty Officer of the Watch.

"Good afternoon, gentlemen. You have been expected by the Captain. He is busy now getting ready to leave the port but he sends his greetings. You are invited to join him for dinner on the navigation level just aft of the bridge at 1730 hours," said the Officer of the Watch.

"Excellent," said Ramsey in his best imitation of an insurance adjustor. Iron Hand saluted with his right hand the Officer of the Watch; as he and Ramsey then followed a crewman to their cabins on the observation level. Iron Hand liked the feel and sound of the tanker as it was preparing to get underway.

Once inside his cabin, Iron Hand ran a quick security check for hidden microphones or listening bugs with the detector that was hidden inside his electric shaver. This was standard CIA procedure for every field officer. After getting an all-clear from his detector, Iron Hand retrieved his Beretta pistol and checked the action plus his extra clips of ammunition. Everything was in perfect working order. Iron Hand pulled back the slide action on his pistol and ran a bullet into the chamber so that he was ready for instant action if necessary. Something in the back of his mind said to get ready for unforeseen happenstances. Iron Hand could not put his finger on his concern, but it was there and he was listening to his senses. He had learned the hard way that this would be the best way to guarantee his survival during the next few days. After all this traveling and action, he decided to take a rest for thirty minutes before getting dressed for dinner with the Captain. During Iron Hand's little nap, the

Basra Queen slipped out of Limassol and began its trip to Marseilles.

*   *   *

"Thank you, Captain Ghadi, for inviting us to join you for dinner," said McQuesten as he and Ramsey settled into their chairs around the dinner table. Three stewards dressed in white serving jackets were standing to the side awaiting instructions to begin serving the meal. Joining the dinner table was the First Lieutenant and the Engineering Officer. Captain Ghadi had a bank of telephones next to his chair to communicate with the bridge in the event of any emergency. The First Officer, Hoshyar al-Sadr, was standing the bridge watch during this dinner service. Seated across from the Captain, Iron Hand guessed Ghadi stood about five feet ten inches with obvious upper-body strength from pumping iron during the long days at sea. Ghadi's well tanned face had a chiseled look, with gray wavy hair and a dark mustache which gave him the looks of an Arab movie star. Flashing dark eyes rounded out his facial appearance. Iron Hand assumed that Ghafi was accustomed to having women throw themselves at his feet when he walked into a room.

The table conversation was routine and the dinner continued on for ninety minutes after which time Ghadi signaled the stewards to clear the table. Black coffee was offered to all those seated at the table.

After finishing his last cup of coffee and getting up from the table, the First Lieutenant walked up to Ramsey and McQuesten and said quietly,

"Come join me on the deck for some fresh air and a cigar if you'd like to smoke after the dinner."

"Certainly," said Ramsey as he looked at McQuesten and wondered if the Captain had told the First Lieutenant to ask them out on the deck. By this time the Captain had excused himself from the table and returned to his duties on the bridge.

After a few moments of silence and checking the deck area, the First Lieutenant sidled up to Ramsey and said,

"You men aren't insurance company representatives, are you?"

"Why do you ask this question, sir?" said Ramsey, wondering what may have tipped off the First Lieutenant to ask such a direct question.

"Why do I ask this question? Neither of you have asked the usual questions about our cargo; how many tons we carry, how many crewmen have come and gone since the last inspection, how many environmental violations we have had written up in port, how many accidents with the crewmen, things of that nature. This is why I am guessing you are not who you claim to be on this voyage."

McQuesten stepped up and looked the man in the eye and said,

"You're correct. We are not insurance brokers that are here to check out what's been going aboard this vessel. We cannot, however, tell you exactly why we are here, but it has to do with vital security concerns. Does the Captain feel the same way about us? Did he ask you to speak to us about our real purpose on board this tanker?"

"No, the Captain did not ask me to speak with you gentlemen," said the First Lieutenant as he again looked around the deck for any crewman lurking nearby trying to listen to their conversations.

"I'll say this much," said the First Lieutenant. "I'm concerned about certain activities going on aboard this ship. I have learned that I'm on a target list of an international police agency. I'm not planning to lose my license and officer qualification papers over any small time smuggling or bill of lading irregularities that may be going on with the Captain or other officers aboard this tanker."

"Would you be willing to tell us more?" asked McQuesten as he moved closer to the First Lieutenant to get a sense of his ability to expand on what he had just passed along. Iron Hand had intensive experience dealing with men who were ready of open up about misdeeds and illicit schemes.

"Yes, but I need to know exactly who you men are and who you are working for," said the First Lieutenant.

Ramsey looked at McQuesten and concurred that it was too risky to blow their cover telling him they were CIA officers. The first lesson learned by CIA field officer is that one never discloses his cover story. It was too risky to break cover, even though this man could furnish information they required to smash the Russian crime syndicate.

"We work closely with a large international police agency. That is all we can disclose at the moment," said McQuesten, as he looked directly at the First Lieutenant.

"I guessed you men might be with Interpol," said the First Lieutenant.

"We cannot deny or confirm that assumption. But we can say that we are here to find answers to what has been going on aboard this tanker and others like it. Anything you agree to tell us will be held in strict confidence and not used against you," said Ramsey.

"All right, I need to talk, so I'll trust you men. As I said, I'm not going to allow myself to get busted and lose my license over a small time smuggling operation."

"Okay, tell us what's bothering you about the Captain or the other officers," said McQuesten as he changed his mood and became serious. "We are all ears to hear what you've got to say."

"Just before the Basra Queen left the pier, two men, who appeared to be Russians, came aboard carrying three black briefcases. They seemed heavy by the way the men were lugging them up the ladders to the Captain's stateroom, which is just aft of the bridge. The visitors remained on board about twenty minutes and left the ship empty handed. There was a large black chauffeured SUV waiting for them on the pier. The climbed into the back seats and drove off quickly. I recognized one of the men because he has come aboard our tanker on one of our previous visits to Limassol."

"Did Captain Ghadi say anything about these two men?" asked McQuesten, as he let the new information sink into his mind, and then asked, "What do you suspect was in the three briefcases?", moving closer. Iron Hand talked almost in a whisper to the First Lieutenant so no one could overhear their conversation.

"As you probably already know, Cyprus is crawling with Russians. There are at least two thousand companies here with origins going back to the old USSR, most dealing in drug trafficking or some kind of hi-tech weapons smuggled from Russia. The money used to pay for these transactions is processed through banks in Nicosia, which easily launder the dirty money through French banks in Marseilles. I'm guessing the briefcases contained diamonds, drugs or counterfeit American currency. Captain Ghadi would be serving as a courier to avoid French customs authorities. Ghadi has said nothing to me about the two men who visited him before we left port. And he never would say anything about the private deals he makes in the various ports of call."

"This is excellent information. If there are any problems for you, we will make sure that the right people know you have cooperated with us. Is there anything else?" asked McQuesten; as he was thinking this information could be used to blow the Russians in Marseilles out of the water for keeps.

"No, there is nothing more I can tell you about this trip to Marseilles," said the First Lieutenant.

"You have been very helpful. Do not worry that your information will be used to compromise your Officer papers," said McQuesten.

*   *   *

Ramsey and McQuesten returned to their cabin and analyzed their situation. Barely out the Cyprus Port of Limassol, they had a virtual gold mine of information dropped into their lap that needed to be passed along to the French port authorities in Marseilles. Now the question was: whom could they trust? The Russians in Marseilles were smart enough to bribe the port inspectors, so news of a plan to apprehend the smugglers would be channeled immediately to the Russians. This would short circuit any opportunity of nailing the criminals when they came to pick up the contents of the three briefcases.

Ramsey and McQuesten holed up in their cabin out of sight for the next few hours and thought through their situation. If the Captain suspected they were wise to one of his smuggling schemes he could easily order his roughneck crewmen to quietly eliminate them and dump their bodies overboard. The French intelligence services had to be alerted ASAP. Regardless of the weakening French political relationship with the current US Administration, the respective intelligence services of the two countries had continued to cooperate. The General Directorate for External Security (DGSE) and the French Counter-Espionage Service (DST) were definite possibilities to work through to arrest the Russians in Marseilles. The question was how to contact them. Also, Interpol might be used, even though Ramsey suspected there was a leak within Interpol.

McQuesten thought perhaps it was time to call head-quarters with his special high-energy battery cell phone with a new GPS capability. McQuesten stepped out on to the deck area near his cabin door. He punched in his secret telephone numbers. In two minutes, contact was made with the satellite orbiting twenty-six miles overhead and it immediately began relaying his call into Langley.

"So what's going to happen?" asked Ramsey, when Iron Hand came back to the cabin after his cell phone call. They both felt it was best to stay put in their cabin as the tanker plowed through the Mediterranean Sea. Langley would handle the reception of the Basra Queen in Marseilles from this point. Iron Hand expected a call from headquarters to alert them to the operational plan after the tanker tied up in Marseilles.

"For now, we have to lie low and play it straight. If the First Lieutenant doesn't panic and blow our cover to the Captain we should be all right. The next eight to ten hours should be the toughest. After that time we should be okay," said Iron Hand. "Also, we should have heard from Langley about what their plans to alert the port authorities in Marseilles."

"Sounds good, let's get some sleep. I'm dead on my feet," said Ramsey.

"Agreed," said Iron Hand but then he added, "Keep your weapon handy in case we get mid night visitors."

*   *   *

At 0630 hours a steady knocking on McQuesten's cabin door started his day. McQuesten knew Ramsey would never knock in such a manner. Iron Hand pulled his Beretta from this shoulder holster, which had been draped over the chair next to his bed. He checked the safety switch and leaned against the steel bulkhead next to the door.

"Yes."

"Sir, this is the First Lieutenant. We need to talk. Please open your door quickly."

"Are you alone?"

"Yes, I am alone. Please open the door."

Iron Hand released the lock and twisted the door knob. The First Lieutenant stepped into the cabin and closed the door quickly but quietly. His face was flushed and his manner nervous.

"Somehow the Captain has become suspicious of you men. Was there communications between you and some shore-based facility last night? The radio operator picked up a transmission and monitored traffic from the Basra Queen. The Captain has strict rules about any unauthorized messages being sent from the ship. The Captain now feels you are policemen trying to prove something against him. It is possible he may send crewmen up here to your cabins to search and investigate the matter. I've seen him act like this with other passengers. When he's mad it's not a pretty thing to witness. On one passage a passenger the Captain had suspicions about was killed by two crewmen and his body thrown overboard. The Captain signed papers during the investigation that the man had been drinking and fell overboard at night. I'm now worried about my safety. You two should be prepared for the worst."

Hearing this warning, Iron Hand summoned Ramsey to his cabin. They conferred about the situation and their precarious position; two CIA officers, outnumbered and probably out-gunned on a tanker in the Mediterranean with no back-up.

The First Lieutenant looked at Iron Hand and said,

"Can either of you fly a helicopter?"

"Yes, I can operate one," said Ramsey. "Is there one aboard the tanker?"

"Yes, it is under my departmental control. Its hanger is on the stern. We could quietly roll it out for a mock inspection and warm it up without drawing too much attention. This is standard procedure right after we leave any port of call. The crewmen wouldn't be alarmed if they saw us. We could easily leave the ship in the helicopter. It has a range of three-hundred eighty nautical miles if the fuel tanks are filled to their capacity plus a thirty minute fuel reserve.

"Let's go look at this bird," said Iron Hand.

The three men carefully exited the cabin, checked for crewmen in the passageway and began their determined walk to the helicopter hanger on the stern of the tanker.

*   *   *

"I want to be on the pier when the Basra Queen ties up with our oil and those three cases of diamonds," said Zhukov to his number two man.

"Do you wish to have extra security because of the diamond delivery?" asked Zhukov's number-two man.

"No, five men, our driver and I will meet the ship. Any more will only raise suspicions and call too much attention to ourselves," said Zhukov who was trying to justify making this pick-up personally. He knew he was violating one of his management precepts by getting too involved in direct action. Normally he sent one of his trusted assistants, but something told him to take charge and handle this job himself. This was going against his management style but he did it anyway.

"As you have ordered, I will arrange everything and double check the ETA of the Basra Queen," said the number two man.

"Very well, keep me posted on any news about this ship's arrival."

*   *   *

"This report from Iron Hand and Ramsey is good news, however I'm not comfortable with two of our best men riding alone on an Iraqi oil tanker in the middle of the Med. I want you to call Navy Operations and tell them to track down the tanker and lock-on to its course and speed. Then have some of our assets tail that tanker as she goes to Marseilles. This shouldn't be much of a problem for our Sixth Fleet. It might give them something important to do that's not just another drill," said the DCI to Tilghman as he sat in the massive office of the DCI.

"I'll get on it immediately. That's a great idea," said Tilghman.

"All right, then see to it, and keep me informed. Make any adjustments to this action plan that you feel are necessary."

Tilghman got on his telephone to the Pentagon. In less than five minutes after the DCI had issued his orders, the Navy Operations Center had begun to put his plan into motion.

"What assets do we have underway in the Mediterranean right now, as we speak?" asked Tilghman of the OpsCenter Watch Officer, who was a four-stripe officer.

"The Harry Truman carrier is seventy miles south-by-southwest of Crete with a screen of five destroyers headed for Yankee Station, one hundred miles south of Cyprus, sir."

"This sounds real good. We need some air cover over an Iraqi tanker named the Basra Queen headed for Marseilles. I don't want any close fly-bys but only shadowing from twenty-five miles. We have two of our best officers aboard this vessel with no back-up and there could be a problem. Do we have any subs that could come up for a rescue pick-up if required?" asked Tilghman.

"We have two subs in port at Naples and one on routine patrol with the USS Truman carrier group, sir," said the Naval Operations Watch Officer.

"This is getting even better. See if you can direct the sub to shadow the Basra Queen from close range until we are sure our men are out of danger. Maybe a little temporary duty away from the carrier group will enliven the duty for the sub skipper. Please set this up ASAP and then get back to me when you have some news," said Tilghman.

*   *   *

The Juan les-Pins Affair

12

McQuesten, Ramsey and the First Liettenant stayed close to the passageway bulkhead to avoid being seen by the crew working with the helicopter. McQuesten looked to the First Lieutenant and said, "You're sure the Captain didn't order this chopper to be rolled out?"

"Yes, I'm sure. This is just a standard drill to verify its readiness. This is done after leaving every port of call. If a member of the crew falls overboard we must try and rescue him with this helicopter."

McQuesten looked back at Ramsey and asked,

"Will you have any problem flying it?"

"No, I've flown this Sikorsky S-76A model before. It should be a piece of cake."

"After the crewmen fire up the engine we'll make our move. I don't want to hang around here any longer than necessary," said McQuesten. It seemed like the helicopter deck hands were taking an eternity to get the chopper ready for its routine preflight check-off list. Apparently this drill had become such a routine there wasn't a sense of urgency to preflight check the helicopter. McQuesten wasn't sure if the crewmen had observed their presence as they braced themselves by the aft passageway bulkhead.

"What is the range of this chopper again?" asked Ramsey, and then he added, "I think our closest point of land is Crete, but I'm not sure how far it is."

"If the fuel tanks are full, we should be able to travel three hundred miles. I know this isn't good planning, but I'm afraid we'll be like so much dead meat if we stay aboard this tanker to argue with the Captain," said the First Lieutenant.

"I agree," said McQuesten as he felt the tension in his voice and a tightening of his neck muscles.

Several deck hands tied down the landing carriage of the helicopter and a third man started winding up the engine. In a few moments the engine was purring like a sewing machine. The man who started the engine locked down the controls and the helicopter began to idle as he left the cockpit and walked to the back of the helicopter to check on the rear rotor blades.

"Okay, it's game time. Let's go look at this bird," said McQuesten.

Ramsey, McQuesten and the ship's officer eased down a short ladder of six steps to the deck where the chopper was tied down. They walked directly to the open cockpit and the First Lieutenant went back to speak to the crewman near the rear rotor blades. Ramsey climbed into the pilot's seat and began to familiarize himself with the controls and gauges. Iron Hand was riding shot-gun next to him. He had already checked his pistol at least three times to make sure it was ready for action. Iron Hand leaned out of the chopper door to see what the First Lieutenant was doing. If he didn't come soon, Iron Hand was ready to tell Ramsey to take off without him. Iron Hand could only imagine some crewmen coming up the deck with weapons ordering them out of the chopper. The cockpit door remained open for the First Lieutenant. He slowly walked back to the door and climbed in the back seat, after releasing all the chocks on the landing carriage. Iron Hand had studied the First Lieutenant carefully, wondering what he had said because the crewmen waved good-bye and smiled as they prepared to lift off the deck. The First Lieutenant climbed casually into the chopper's cockpit and sat back in the rear seat.

"I told them we were going back to Limassol to pick up three commissary crewmen who missed the ship's movement," said the First Lieutenant.

"You must have convinced them because they didn't look concerned when we climbed aboard," said Ramsey.

"Yeah, they're good men. They'll believe anything I tell them."

Ramsey increased the RPMs of the chopper and eased back on the control stick. The helicopter jumped into the air and moved smartly out over the sea below. Iron Hand looked back at the tanker as they steadied up on a course toward Crete. Ramsey appeared comfortable at the controls. Their air speed was 100 knots. The question now became one of stretching the fuel supply. McQuesten began to wonder what the Captain was thinking after he saw the helicopter leaving the stern of the tanker. Ramsey looked at McQuesten and said,

"Maybe you should check-in with headquarters or the Sixth Fleet and bring them up to speed about our situation."

"Ramsey, you're on the money with that thought. I was just thinking the same thing," answered Iron Hand as he pumped his fist in the air.

McQuesten reached into his pocket and pulled out his special cell phone. He started dialing the numbers for a satellite hook-up and a relay line-feed back to Langley. As he waited for his call to go through he double-checked the GPS readings so he could pin point their location for the call. In a few minutes he heard a telephone ringing halfway across the world. "My God, I love modern technology."

*   *   *

Aboard the nuclear-powered carrier the USS Harry Truman, CVN-75, a lieutenant junior grade sat at the Communication Watch Officer's desk in the radio shack processing routine communication traffic. The radio shack, or radio one, was located one deck below the flight deck. The USS Truman was one thousand eighty-eight feet long, displacing ninety-one thousand three hundred tons and its four screws were capable of producing speeds in excess of thirty-five knots. The USS Truman carried a crew of five thousand six-hundred-plus men and women to service the air group. The noise created by the heavy jet planes landing, the recycling of the four steam catapults and landing wires made the radio shack extremely noisy. A first class radio operator shouted at the CWO,

"Flash message coming through from CNO, Naval Warfare Operations for Commander Carrier Task Force Group 66.6."

The CWO jumped up from his desk and ran to the Fleet radio computer printer and watched the coded five letter message groups coming through. He tried to guess how long the message was going to be and how long it would take to decode it. He returned to his desk and called the Communications Officer in Flag Plot.

"Sir, we have a coded Flash message for the Admiral coming through as we speak. I wanted to alert you that we will begin decoding it immediately."

"Very well, keep me posted. I will alert the Admiral and send a staff officer to assist you in the radio shack," said the Flag Communications Officer.

Ten minutes later the decoded message was being read by the Admiral as he was seated in his Flag Plot bridge chair high above the flight deck of the USS Truman. It read:

"Commander Carrier Task Force 66.6 detach sub from carrier group. Submarine to be ordered to proceed at top speed to locate and shadow tanker Basra Queen believed to be steaming from Cyprus on course for Marseilles. Commander CARDIV 66.6 to launch S-3 Viking COD aircraft for search of same tanker and possible rescue of two CIA Officers plus passenger now flying helicopter on course 340 degrees speed 100 knots toward Crete. Helicopter fuel may be critical. S-3 Viking to orbit helicopter until passenger's disposition is assured. Advise CNO, Naval warfare operations via Flash message when action is underway."

*   *   *

Iron Hand's cell phone came to life. He punched in his security code numbers, said hello, and listened.

"Iron Hand, this is Flag Communication Officer for Naval Task Force 66.6 Alter your flight course and steer vector zero four five magnetic to bring your flight to rendezvous with rescue vessel currently underway. S-3 Viking COD aircraft also on rendezvous course to drop inflatable life boat craft if necessary. Stand by this channel for further traffic. Acknowledge."

"This is Iron Hand. Acknowledged, Out."

Iron Hand looked at Ramsey and said,

"Help is on the way. I hope our fuel holds out until we are in direct visual contact with our rescue squad. Let's put on those life jackets just in case we are forced to ditch before the good-guys show up."

After approximately fifteen minutes of flying the course of zero four five magnetic a message came over the radio frequency the helicopter was guarding.

"S-76 Sikorsky chopper, this is S-3B Viking aircraft orbiting above you. Please acknowledge that you copy this transmission, Over."

"S-3B Viking this is S-76 chopper. We read you loud and clear. Do not have you on visual. Over," said Ramsey.

"S-76 chopper, please follow these course changes. Steer new vector two seven zero which will put you on rendezvous Commander CARDIV 66.6. Be prepared to land aboard Mule Skinner and transfer all passengers to COD for next destination. Rendezvous approximately one hundred miles. Is fuel sufficient for this trip? Over."

"This is S-76 chopper. Roger your last S-3B Viking. Coming up on two seven zero. Fuel satisfactory for one hundred miles. Roger, out," said Ramsey.

*   *   *

As Iron Hand relaxed, his mind began to formulate ideas and plans for the confrontation with the Russian mobsters in Marseilles. A leak from the port authorities would negate any advantage that he might have at the outset of their operation. Iron Hand wondered if Ghadi would be able to piece together all that had happened or would he just proceed on to Marseilles. Letting the chips fall as they may would be Ghadi's best option, thought Iron Hand. The Captain of a ship is supposed to take care of the ship and crew. Protecting himself should be secondary. If he could assist the Russians with the three cases of contraband, it would be a secondary thought. Perhaps Ghadi would use the contents of the briefcases for his own purposes: a little game of double-cross on the high seas? Who would know what really had happened? Iron Hand closed his eyes and let his mind sift through all the action of the last ten days. Goodbody's face came to mind. He wondered what she might be doing. Was she safe? Could a French gang be attempting to even the score with her for tipping off the CIA and Interpol? Finally, Iron Hand relaxed, settled back in his seat and fell into a deep sleep with the sound of the whirling rotor blades ringing in his ears.

*　　　*　　　*

The radio man in the tanker communications room continued to monitor the voice communication frequencies used aboard the S-76 chopper. His squawk box came to life when Captain Ghadi called,

"Radio room, this is the Captain. Do you have any new information about the stolen helicopter?"

"We believe they have made contact with US Navy vessels and are planning to land the helicopter on one of their ships not too far from our position. We do not have the S-76 on radar at this time, Captain."

"Very well, keep listening on that frequency. Advise me immediately if you hear any new traffic."

"Yes, sir," said the radio operator.

Ghadi settled back in his elevated chair on the bridge and let his eyes scan the sea. He noticed it was beginning to produce some swells. The Mediterranean Sea could stir up and become ugly very quickly. He had the urge to light up one of his favorite Egyptian cigarettes. His mind was tugging at the accustomed lifestyle issues that he was not anxious to see disappear. He began to mull over the possibilities. What were his best options now? Why did the First Lieutenant and the two imposters leave the ship? Why did the two men come aboard in the first place? Ghadi's mind sorted through the pluses and minuses; attempting to visualize his survival percentages after the Basra Queen was docked in Marseilles. He had the three briefcases of smuggled diamonds securely locked in his cabin. His tanker also carried the usual quarter million extra gallons of Iraqi oil for Saddam Hussein's Oil Ministry. Should he use his cell phone to contact the Russian, Yuri, or should he ignore the obvious risks and pretend that nothing has happened? The Basra Queen steamed through the sea at fifteen knots giving him an ETA in Marseilles of slightly more than three days. Assuming the weather held and there were no mechanical breakdowns the tanker could maintain this speed. Ghadi continued to speculate about his future as a ship captain if the French port authorities searched the tanker for contraband and then found his cargo bill of lading to be fraudulent. He was not interested in becoming a notorious disgraced tanker captain like Mr. Hazelwood who had commanded the Exxon-Valdez. He visualized himself sitting in a street-side café in Paris sipping a glass of chardonnay and watching the beautiful women walk by his table.

*   *   *

Ramsey eased the S-76 Sikorsky helicopter for a landing on the number one elevator platform of the USS Harry Truman.

"Welcome aboard the Truman, gentlemen. What do you want done with this chopper?" asked the Flight Deck Air Operations Officer. Iron Hand saluted the Officer and said,

"We have no further use for it. We suggest that you stow it below and off-load it at the first port-of-call. The First Lieutenant here will provide you all the ownership details. We borrowed this bird from an oil tanker about one hundred and fifty miles from our present position."

"Okay, sir. We can handle everything from here. Suggest you report to the Air Operations Officer. He is already working on the transportation that you want to Marseilles," said the Flight Deck Air Operations Officer. Iron Hand and Ramsey went to the Truman's conning tower island and worked their way up three deck levels to the Air Operations center.

"Sir, please say hello to Brad Ramsey. I am Jack McQuesten. Our mission is to neutralize a Russian money laundering operation in Marseilles. We need a change of clothes, some chow and then a flight to Marseilles ASAP. Can we work this out?" asked Iron Hand.

"Sir, we are under orders from the Naval Warfare Operations Center in Washington, DC to cooperate fully with any of your requests. We have an S-3 Viking fueled and standing by. The flight time to Marseilles should be three hours after take-off from the Truman," said the Air Operations Officer.

"Sounds like music," said Ramsey. Iron Hand nodded his approval. The three men left the Air Operations center of the USS Truman and followed a Marine below decks to the Ward Room. The Executive Officer greeted them and arranged for new clothing and hot food prior to their launch in the S-3 Viking. The officers aboard the USS Truman were so cooperative that McQuesten was tempted to break his cover and tell them this was a CIA operation. But he knew that it was not smart and against all his training and standing instructions not to open up to people, even to members of your own team.

Zhukov sat behind his desk as he focused on his agenda. The private intercom on his desk buzzed twice. This signaled that Bruslov had arrived for his interview and was waiting in the outside office. Zhukov's mind snapped to attention. He set aside files and straightened up some old correspondence. He opened a journal and placed a pen nearby so he could jot down notes. He pushed the intercom button once which signaled he was ready for Bruslov.

Zhukov rose up from his chair and stood behind his desk. He smiled and extended his hand to Bruslov when he was ushered into his office.

"Welcome to our company," said Zhukov.

"Thank you for inviting me to see you."

Zhukov's assistant motioned that he would leave. Zhukov nodded his approval. The two Russians were now alone.

Zhukov took a few moments to study this young man. He cleared his mind. The first impressions were good. He began the interview, saying.

"We have been looking for new blood for our Juan les-Pins operation. I'm afraid our work isn't as exciting as atomic warheads for the Russian army."

"That was my past. I'm glad to be done with that part of my life."

"I'm sure that you are. What do you think you can bring to us," asked Zhukov as he sank into his chair looking straight at Bruslov.

"I've had experience dealing with Egyptian Muslims and al-Qaeda cell leaders in London. I speak fluent English and Russian. The American FBI arrested me after an aborted mission in the States. A Russian attorney in Brighton Beach represented me. He and some Russian associates worked hard to get me free. I owe them many favors. If not for their work, I'd still be serving time in prison."

"Sounds like you got lucky. I am sure you could handle yourself well in Juan les-Pins after your time in the Russian army. We have many business contacts in the Middle East, particularly Cyprus. We're beginning to become active in the trading of diamonds and weapons. Trading oil here in Marseilles is our main thrust."

Bruslov listened carefully to Zhukov. He didn't want to appear too anxious. He chose his words carefully when he responded to Zhukov's questions.

"Weapons are no problem. I'm familiar with most Russian equipment. Diamonds and oil are new subjects for me, but I'm sure I could learn quickly."

Bruslov stopped talking. He didn't want to be caught saying too much. He wanted to learn about Zhukov and his trading operation. Bruslov knew he wouldn't learn anything by talking. Zhukov picked up the conversation, saying,

"I'm sure you could. Currently, most of our business is gambling related in Juan les-Pins. We're quietly expanding into trading with Muslims who want to purchase guns and explosives. We usually accept only cash; Euros and American currency. Occasionally, we accept diamonds in payment for weapons. Recently we have taken calls from Russians who offer to sell us stolen weapons from army depots. We also get offered weapons captured from warlord militias who have been put out of business. We have a policy to generally take things slow. We never rush into any deals. We are not like Adnan Khashoggi who does big weapons deals throughout the Middle East. We have to know with whom we are dealing. We don't want to become victims of an Interpol sting operation."

Zhukov picked up his pen and jotted down a few notes; he liked this young Russian. His scrape with the Americans didn't bother Zhukov in the least. It made him feel just that more comfortable. "It's a little early in the day, but would you like to join me with a glass of vodka? It's an excellent brand," said Zhukov. Bruslov hesitated, but agreed to a drink with the man who might soon be his boss. Bruslov wasn't a drinking man but he knew Russians traditionally liked to seal a deal by drinking vodka. "Yes, I'd enjoy a glass."

Zhyukov walked to his private bar and carefully poured a shot of vodka into two crystal glasses. He passed a glass to Bruslov, raised his glassa and said,

"Za vashe zhorov'ye!"

Bruslov raised his glass and replied,

"Yes, to your health."

Zhukov drained his glass of vodka, returned to his desk chair, sat down and looked at Bruslov. "How would you like to join our organization?"

"I would be pleased to do so," replied Bruslov, who was surprised a job offer came so quickly.

"We can offer you seven thousand Euros a month to start. Perhaps more after you become familiar with our operation."

"Seven thousand per month would be fine," as a swell of relief came over Bruslov. "When would I start?"

"You start today."

"Excellent."

"One thing you must learn about me and our organization is that we can move fast if we are sure of ourselves. I have an important job coming up in a day or so. I want you to come along when I lead a group of men to pick up a delivery of diamonds from Cyprus. This will give you a chance to see our men in action."

"What should I do next?" asked Bruslov.

"Go to a hotel and check-in. We can assist you in finding an apartment later this week. Be back here tomorrow at eight in the morning. We can get you set up here for some orientation before you go to Juan les-Pins."

Bruslov got up from his chair and saluted Zhukov as he turned to leave the office. Zhukov returned the friendly salute and returned to his paper work on his desk. After a few moments Zhukov returned to his bar and poured another shot of vodka into his glass.

Zhukov sat at his desk nursing the glass of vodka while he reluctantly made the decision to get directly involved in the diamond delivery from the Basra Queen. This decision was a departure from his usual management style. Normally, Zhukov would delegate a job like this to a trusted second in command. This delivery of diamonds, however, had caused him apprehension from the outset. He sensed this transaction wouldn't be business as usual. He attempted to analyze the potential problems with this diamond delivery. If the port authorities and Interpol had the tanker under surveillance, driving on the pier directly to the tanker in a SUV was out of the question. Zhukov sat quietly and continued to let his mind work out a plan down to the smallest details. Nothing about his plan was hammered in stone. Anything could cause him to adjust his plans. He would remain flexible. His decision to bring his newest associate, Sergei Bruslov, along on this job gave him some comfort. He embraced the idea of including the young Russian. He felt Bruslov could be trusted.

* * *

Captain Ghadi snapped out of his extended reverie. "Those two imposters are law enforcement men from Interpol or the American CIA. They are attempting to nail me on smuggling charges. I must create a diversion in port to make it easier to get these diamonds to the Russians. My transmissions are certainly being monitored. I must contact the Russian in Cyprus, Yuri, and instruct him to tell his counterpart in Marseilles how to take delivery of the diamonds." Ghadi reached for a pen and scratched out a message he would transmit by radio telephone to the Russian, "Yuri, pick up the three briefcases by water taxi from lowered starboard side ladder. Do not board the tanker from the pier. Suggest a pick-up time of 2100 hours. Ghadi." Ghadi then thought to himself: too further confuse any law enforcement personnel I will arrange for a large delivery of food stuffs for 1800 hours and invite all port authority officials to an open-house dinner reception at 1700 hours.

All this activity near the Basra Queen will confuse anyone performing surveillance. Ghadi seemed to rest a little easier in his captain's chair, after coming up with this in-port diversion plan of action.

*   *   *

Zhukov looked at his telephone notes after talking with Yuri in Cyprus: "Send your men to the tanker via boat to the starboard side ladder; pick up the diamonds at 2100 hours."

Zhukov wondered why the change of plans? Why not continue with the usual operational activity of a late night visit by his trusted men in a SUV? I want those diamonds delivered without any hassles. The captain of the tanker must be suspicious about something. Perhaps someone has tipped him off about a surveillance plot. Should I set-up a contingency plan? I do not want to walk into a law-enforcement trap. Zhukov picked up his glass of vodka and sipped a taste of the liquor. He let his mind run through all the problems he could foresee. Pick up the diamonds in a boat on the starboard side of the tanker: what kind of boat? How many boats? Zhukov thought that perhaps he could bribe his port authority contacts to supply two boats from the Harbor Master. These boats would look official and not raise any suspicion as they came alongside the Basra Queen. Zhukov wrote down on his paper: good idea! Check this out carefully. Zhukov sat back in his chair. He took another sip of vodka. A nagging thought crept into Zhukov's mind; maybe the American CIA had put up the Captain to change the delivery instructions so they could capture him with the diamonds in the harbor. Perhaps being on a boat was too risky. Zhukov continued to mull over his options.

*   *   *

Iron Hand and Ramsey sat in their Marseilles hotel room, and continued to work on their plan of action against the Russian crime syndicate.

"We can't go to the French port authorities yet. I'd bet my next paycheck that the Russian gangsters have spies in the port authority, and our plan would be tipped off to the bad-guys immediately after we made our strategy known," said Iron Hand.

Ramsey nodded in agreement, sipped his coffee and said, "I can check with the port authority and get the ETA of the tanker. Also, which berth she had been assigned."

Iron Hand sat in his chair and let his mind roll through the problems he faced.

"What about Interpol? What about notifying the DST? Shouldn't we plug them in at this time? Look at the size of this harbor. We are going to need help if we expect to pull this off successfully."

"Yes, I agree. I have a trustworthy Interpol contact here in Marseilles. He is a very solid individual. I can alert him that we will need the assistance and a few trustworthy Interpol officers. I know he'll be able to help us," said Ramsey.

"Here's another thought. We're going to require water transportation: a fast boat driven by a Frenchman who knows the harbor. Ask your Interpol contact if he can line-up a fast boat and a good driver," said Iron Hand.

"Okay, that shouldn't be a problem. How much time do we have before the tanker arrives?" asked Ramsey.

"I'm guessing about five hours."

Iron Hand continued to study his notes and a chart of the harbor. The possibilities of failure were large given the size of the tanker and the men involved.

"We've got to get some of our people involved with the oil unloading. I'm betting the tanker has extra oil "top-loaded" that they will attempt to pump off after the legitimate oil cargo is delivered to the tank farm. We'll need someone who can tell us when the contraband starts flowing and where it goes."

Iron Hand looked at Ramsey and said,

"Your Interpol contact has five hours to line-up reliable people who can follow the oil through the terminal pipeline and calculate the tonnage of contraband. Someone who can figure out how the Russian crime syndicate has corrupted the system: someone clever."

"Let's focus on the power boat. Here's my plan: we wait in a car on the pier, with our lights out, in a location that gives us a clear view of the tanker after she has tied up. We must be in radio contact with the fast-boat driver so we can call him to pick us up quickly. While in our car, we'll watch for the bad-guys to show up on the pier in a van. We must also station Interpol officers along the pier with good views fore and aft, port and starboard, of the Basra Queen. We may need to station a few Interpol officers at the bow area of the tanker so they have a clear view down the starboard side. We'll also need two trucks positioned to block off the pier exits. We can seal off the entire area on the pier. Our prey will be surrounded. We can nail them with the goods in the three briefcases that the First Lieutenant told us about. How does all this sound for a beginning?" asked Iron Hand.

"I like it," answered Ramsey.

*   *   *

As the Basra Queen slowly moved closer to the pier, two tug boats began to push the bow toward her berth. Deck hands were standing ready and awaiting orders to heave lines from the tanker to the men on the pier. Slowly the docking operation unfolded as the tugs pushed the tanker to the pier. Iron Hand and Ramsey, sitting in a black sedan at the head of the pier, could easily see Ghadi standing on the bridge, issuing orders to the crewmen on deck of the tanker.

"The last time we were near this ship Ghadi had us at his mercy. Now I'm feeling a lot better about our odds. I think that Ghadi knows he is 'in our house now' as the saying goes," said Iron Hand as he checked his watch and recorded in his mind, 1730 hours. "I don't think anything will happen until after dark and the tanker is well into the process of unloading its oil cargo."

"You are probably right with that assessment," said Ramsey. "But, I'm going to jack up our troops to keep an eye peeled for any Russians arriving on the dock in a SUV."

"Good idea, give them a little pep-talk. Tell them not to go to sleep. The party's just about to begin," said Iron Hand.

*   *   *

Zhukov peered out of the window of his BMW sports utility vehicle at his men on the next pier where the tanker was moored. Immediately below them were two thirty-foot Harbor Master launches used to visit ships coming into the Marseilles port. Zhukov was dressed in black pants with expensive deck shoes. A dark rubberized jacket complete with a hood covered his torso in case of inclement weather. He also wore a tight-fitting billed hat. He was determined to dress the part of a commander leading his troops on an important mission. Hidden in his belt was a holster that held a nine millimeter fully-automatic Luger pistol. He hadn't fired a gun for years but he felt good carrying the sidearm. Zhukov thought his men would have more respect if they saw he was armed and ready for action. The time was now 1830 hours. Zhukov had eaten a light dinner but he planned to eat again after the three cases of diamonds were in the safe at his office. Now the waiting game began until 2100 hours. Then he would make a slow approach in a motor launch to the starboard side of the tanker. Zhukov had already ordered two of his men to drive to the docking area of the tanker to confirm that an extended ladder was lowered in position along the starboard side of the ship. Bruslov sat in the rear of the SUV, watching Zhukov's every move. He was dressed similarly to Zhukov but he wasn't carrying a weapon.

*   *   *

Iron Hand continued his vigil; there was little talking between him and Ramsey. As the time slowly passed, Iron Hand fought the temptation to brazenly board the huge tanker and confront Ghadi. He knew, of course that would be a big mistake. Iron Hand had set his trap but now he wasn't sure who would end up in his snare. The prize was three briefcases of drugs, diamonds or counterfeit American currency, according to the First Lieutenant, who had long since left Marseilles. He had done his job and was now looking for a new billet.

Iron Hand thought to himself; this entire operation was the result of the First Lieutenant giving them the information about the three briefcases. What if this turned out to be a wild goose chase? What if this was just an elaborate ruse? Everything depended on the information that the First Lieutenant had passed along. Now he was gone.

An Interpol look-out near the stern of the Basra Queen broke the silence with a report. "Small craft approaching stern of the tanker; looks like a Harbor Master boat checking for lines or waste being dumped from the ship. Its moving very slowly but with some purpose; I count at least five men standing in the aft end of the boat."

"Good report, Look-Out. Keep us posted," said Ramsey as he glanced at Iron Hand and pumped his fist, to register his feeling that now we're getting somewhere.

"All this traffic coming and going on the dockside area is confusing. How can we keep track of all these people and guess who they might be?" said Ramsey.

"You're right," said Iron Hand.

"Call the power boat driver and tell him to pick us up at the end of the pier. We'll meet him down there in three minutes;" Iron Hand checked his watch; it showed 1915 hours. Was this change in location just nervous energy being used up? Iron Hand questioned himself. He hated to sit in one place waiting for action.

After walking through the crowd of crewmen and pier longshoremen, Iron Hand and Ramsey finally got to the ladder which led them down to their power boat. They boarded the boat and ordered the driver to head for the stern of the tanker. Two Harbor Master boats where circling the stern area at a slow speed as if they were killing time.

Iron Hand and Ramsey checked their hand weapons again. There was a good probability that they would need them for a shoot-out with the Russian syndicate muscle men. As they cruised past the Harbor Master boats the men onboard looked rugged, tough and spoiling for a fight. Iron Hand looked at the Frenchman and said,

"Steer past these two boats and head down the starboard side of the tanker." As the powerboat moved forward Iron Hand checked out the deck area which was about sixty feet above the surface of the water. The ladder that was hanging from the main deck was attended by two guards with side arm pistols on their belts. They frowned as they stared down at Iron Hand who had his own game face on and looked straight back at them.

Iron Hand picked up his boat radio telephone that allowed him to communicate directly with all his Interpol look-outs.

"To all units, confirm what you have visually at your posts at this time. Are there any suspicious activities at this time? Please report, over." Nothing was reported back to Iron Hand.

"I think we are on the right track," said Iron Hand as he starred into the night. "Turn this boat around and let's get back into the harbor by the stern of the tanker."

*   *   *

The Juan les-Pins Affair

13

As Zhukov and his men waited near the terminal area by Basra Queen, second thoughts over his boarding strategy crept into his mind. Yes, he embraced a plan revised from his earlier decision. He decided to lead his men up the gangway ladder to board the tanker. He would station a motor launch at the foot of the ladder lowered from the starboard side of the tanker. The motor launch would give them an escape route if trouble developed on the tanker. Since Zhukov never was unsure about any of his decisions, he confidently barked out new orders to the BMW driver, "Proceed to the pier. I will show you where to park." They finally parked near the bow of the tanker next to a huge stack of empty shipping containers. Zhukov's party waited for darkness to settle around the harbor. Then they would go aboard the tanker for the meeting with Captain Ghadi.

Ghadi watched the time slipping by in his quarters as he wondered when Zhukov would make his appearance. Ghadi had also prepared an elaborate personal escape plan to be executed immediately after Zhukov left the tanker. As part of his escape plan, earlier in the day Ghadi shipped several luggage bags full of personal items off the Basra Queen to a very ordinary hotel in downtown Marseilles. He purposely chose a hotel of lesser status to avoid any hotel scrutiny. Once he was on his way to Paris he wanted to leave no trail for Interpol. The strange behavior of the two men posing as insurance inspectors in Cyprus convinced him that they were Interpol officers. As a second part of his escape plan, Ghadi gave orders to his department heads that all non-essential crew members not involved in the oil delivery operation were to be given liberty. He planned to leave the tanker in civilian clothes, hoping that with most of the crew on liberty his departure would go virtually unnoticed. As he waited in his quarters for Zhukov, Ghadi craved a glass of wine but held off because of the importance of this meeting. If all went well, there would be plenty of time later to enjoy good wine. He reached into the desk drawer for a fresh pack of cigarettes. It felt good to light up a cigarette and relax a little under the circumstances. The open house he planned for the huge tanker hadn't drawn many visitors but still provided a modest diversion. He would take full advantage of the visitors walking on the ship.

*　　　　*　　　　*

Iron Hand and Ramsey had been sitting in their motor launch for thirty minutes, approximately one hundred yards off the stern of the tanker. No suspicious activity on the tanker gave Iron Hand any indication that the Russians had gone aboard the tanker. He knew that the game was afoot so it was important to be alert to every possibility. At least from this motor launch he could observe any suspicious persons leaving the tanker in a boat. It would be easy to call in his Interpol officers to meet him along the water front if necessary. Ramsey announced he sighted a power boat moving toward amidships on the starboard side of the tanker. He signaled to Iron Hand to watch its progress.

"Maybe we're finally going to have some action. There's a small motor launch going along the starboard side. It looks like it's going to the boarding ladder. Something is afoot. I like our position here to react to this action," said Ramsey.

Iron Hand, however, was having second thoughts about how they could react from their position to intercept the Russians. "I hope we've made the right move being out here in this power launch," thought Iron Hand, as he focused his binoculars on the starboard side of the tanker. "There's nothing happening on the deck at the top of the ladder."

    *   *   *

Zhukov checked his watch and motioned his men to start moving to the forward brow gangway. He had grown tired of this waiting game. It was time to get moving. Zhukov began to encourage his men.

"All right men, listen up. We will walk along the pier and watch the area for police or Interpol men who may have set trap for us. If all seems well, we will board the tanker and proceed directly to the Captain's quarters. I will do all the talking and negotiating. If there is gun-play don't be afraid to shoot. If our path is blocked to leave the ship from the portside gangway we will go down the starboard ladder to the motor launch. Does everyone understand how this plan is going to unfold?"

There were no questions as the men nodded their understanding. Zhukov motioned the men to carefully start moving toward the forward brow and the gangway boarding ladder. With the open house crowd also moving toward the tanker gangway Zhukov and his men would have little trouble blending into the activity. Zhukov signaled his men by holding up his hand for one last visual inspection looking for police. He found no one that appeared suspicious. Satisfied there was no trap he said, "All right, let's go up the gangway. Follow me." Zhukov led his men up the gang-way to the duty officer. Bruslov tagged along in the rear.

"My name is Zhukov. The Captain is expecting me and my party to visit with him in his cabin. We know the way. There is no need to accompany us," said Zhukov in his best commander's voice.

"Very well, sir. The Captain left word he was expecting you. Please make your way to his quarters on the third level," said the Watch Officer.

Zhukov and his men climbed up the ladders on their way to Ghadi's quarters without further problems. They reached the door to Ghadi's cabin and Zhukov knocked loudly three times. Ghadi must have been tipped off they were on the way by the Deck Watch Officer. Ghadi motioned Zhukov and his men to enter his cabin.

Zhukov sat back in a chair in front of a metal desk that served as Ghadi's office and chart reading table. Zhukov had left his jacket unzipped so he could easily pull out his pistol if he sensed any danger. Zhukov looked nervously at Ghadi and said,

"Let's get down to business. I'm here to pick up the diamonds my partner in Cyprus consigned to you."

"Yes, your partner, Yuri, has paid me well. I'm happy to be dealing directly with you so there'll be no confusion about the delivery," said Ghadi as he smiled and nodded to Zhukov.

Ghadi started to get up from his chair and Zhukov reached for his weapon. He was suspicious that something was about to happen that he hadn't anticipated.

"No need for that, sir. I'm only going to my locker to get the three briefcases which your partner consigned to me. Perhaps one of your men should come with me to bring them to you," said Ghadi as he stood behind his metal desk and waited for an approval of his suggestion.

Zhukov looked to one of his men and nodded his head; however, his right hand remained on his weapon.

"Please come with me," Ghadi said to the guard.

Zhukov never took his eyes from Ghadi as he and the guard moved toward the locker closet. Ghadi reached into his pocket, pulled out a gold key chain, selected the proper key and opened the locker. Inside were three black leather brief cases. Ghadi motioned with his hand for the guard to pick them up and take them to Zhukov.

Zhukov carefully examined each briefcase, opening each one to inspect the contents. There were small cases of diamonds of various sizes. Zhukov made no attempt to inventory the cache of precious stones. Apparently satisfied that the delivery was complete, Zhukov looked at his men, nodded his approval, and turned his attention back to Ghadi saying,

"It appears that our business is done. You have been paid and our job now is to leave your ship without incident. There has been something troubling me about this entire business; however, it now appears that my apprehension was unwarranted. Captain, it has been good doing business with you. Perhaps we will meet again."

"Yes, perhaps we will," said Ghadi anxiously, for he, too, was ready to get this business completed.

Zhukov's men picked up the briefcases and left the cabin. They then made their way down the companionway to the ladders that would take them to the main deck. They would go back down the gangway, and on to the pier.

*   *   *

Iron Hand and Ramsey had been in their motor launch too long. Iron Hand looked at Ramsey and said,

"I don't feel good about being out here. I think that we are missing some action. Let's get back to the pier." Ramsey leaned toward the power boat driver and motioned him to head back to the pier.

The power boat driver sped about one hundred yards to a boat landing next to the pier where the tanker was moored. While the short trip was being made, Iron Hand called his Interpol and DST officers. He ordered them to meet him on the pier near the forward gangway of the tanker. Within a few minutes, Iron Hand and Ramsey plus six Interpol security officers were walking up the gangway. They were met by two men and the duty watch officer. They were informed that no one was allowed to come aboard on official business without permission from the Captain. The Interpol officers showed their inspection warrants and Interpol ID which satisfied the duty officer. One Interpol officer remained on the quarterdeck to ensure that no one alerted the Captain or the Command Duty Officer that Interpol and DST officers had boarded the tanker.

Iron Hand looked at Ramsey and said,

"I'm getting internal vibes that we are about to run into trouble. Spread out these five Interpol men. Tell them to move along the main deck and look for any suspicious men. You and I will stick together and head up the ladder to the Captain's quarters on the third level. It's possible that the Russians are up there right now doing their business. Let's move out."

Iron Hand and Ramsey started up the nearby ladder off the quarterdeck and arrived at the first level. They had just begun to work their way down the companion way when they heard some heavy foot-step traffic coming toward them from the ladder leading down from the third deck. Iron Hand and Ramsey ducked into a rope locker and drew their weapons. Iron Hand pulled back the slide action on his Beretta and unlocked the safety. Two Russian crime syndicate muscle men walked by the rope locker where Iron Hand and Ramsey hid. No one was following closely behind the two men. Iron Hand came up behind the second man and clobbered him on the head. The first man reacted and charged back at Iron Hand and Ramsey. This turned out to be a mistake, as the two CIA officers quickly dispatched him and dragged both men into the rope locker. Iron Hand and Ramsey relieved the men of their weapons and tied them up securely with the available rope. The two Russians would not be going anywhere.

Several moments later, another two lumbering Russians were heard coming down the ladder from the second level. They called out the names of their two comrades that Iron Hand and Ramsey had dispatched. The first man saw Iron Hand and pulled his gun. He made ready to fire when Iron Hand fired one shot in his direction but missed. The Russian fired two wild shots in return and ran back up the ladder to the second level. Now the gun battle was on.

"What's happening?" demanded Zhukov after hearing the shots. One of Zhukov's guards answered, "Two men on the level immediately below here. They appear to be police."

Zhukov frowned at hearing this report. This is the development he had not wanted, but his escape plan with the motor launch on the starboard side would now kick into play.

"Very well then, let's go aft along this passageway and work our way down to the first deck. We will depart from the starboard side ladder to the boat below. Move out!" ordered Zhukov. Zhukov was second in a line of men moving along the passageway toward any ladder that would take them down to the tanker's main deck.

Zhukov and his men walked hurriedly along the passageway as they tried to find a ladder. All the men had guns drawn and were ready to shoot. As they moved along the passageway, Zhukov kept an eye on the men lugging the three briefcases. Perspiration began to roll down Zhukov's body. He badgered himself over his decision to lead his men on this operation.

*   *   *

Ghadi heard the shots ring out from the decks just below his quarters. He assumed that Interpol had come aboard the tanker and waited for Zhukov to pick up the briefcases, arrest him and his gang members. They would probably want to take him into custody with the evidence. Ghadi hurriedly changed into civilian clothes, carefully placed a fake mustache on his lip and donned a dark Homburg felt hat. He picked up his briefcase that was full of cash and a Luger pistol plus extra clips of ammunition. He was prepared to protect himself, but he didn't want to engage in any gun-play with the Russians, Interpol or DST officers. He quietly made his way toward the after-brow quarterdeck which, according to his orders, was being manned by two sailors. Ghadi did not anticipate any problems getting off the tanker and blending into the crowds visiting the tanker or those on the pier. He had made sure that his letter of resignation as Commanding Officer would be easily found in his unlocked cabin. As he walked down the gangway, he felt relief as tension left his body for the first time in weeks. His planning and execution of his escape was working.

Iron Hand's spirits had risen since getting off the motor launch. Being aboard a large ship was more to his liking. Iron Hand and Ramsey moved along the passageway on the second level with guns drawn. Ramsey was right behind him watching their backside, as they sought out the Russians. As they moved along cautiously, a shot rang out, missing them by inches. Iron Hand sensed this was a warning shot fired by a rear-guard Russian telling them to not come closer. Iron Hand carefully moved to the corner of the passageway and peered around the bulkhead. A large man dressed in black clothes stood twenty feet down the passageway next to the bulkhead. He raised his pistol to aim and fire at Iron Hand. Iron Hand dropped to the deck and fired two shots at the man blocking the way. He fell to the deck but did manage to get off a return shot that missed its mark. As Iron Hand and Ramsey rushed by the man on the deck, he appeared dead from his wounds. Iron Hand had no way of knowing how many other men they were up against. At every turn in the passageway there could be another Russian waiting with his weapon drawn.

Iron Hand glanced at his watch: 2230 hours. Where had the time gone? Iron Hand wondered. Ramsey looked at Iron Hand and said,

"How many of these guys are we going to have to take out before we find the head man?" Iron Hand didn't have a clue about how many Russians were on the ship, but he knew that his Interpol officers were on the main deck watching for any suspicious persons retreating from the tanker. The French DST men were positioned on the pier, waiting for any gang members to come their way.

*   *   *

Zhukov had pushed his men along the passageway until they reached a ladder that would take them to the main deck. Visitors still roaming about on the main deck were oblivious to all the shooting and the life and death struggle which was being played out. Zhukov saw the starboard after brow area where the ladder had been lowered to the water below. His mood took a positive turn as he realized he and his men only had to go down the ladder and move out in the motor launch.

"All right men, head over to that quarterdeck area and go down the ladder. Two of you go first. If there is trouble, don't be afraid to use your weapons," said Zhukov. The men proceeded toward the quarterdeck with their weapons in hand but kept them covered just under their shirts. One of the men, upon reaching the quarterdeck turned back and signaled that all was safe for Zhukov and the men carrying the diamonds to come forward.

An Interpol officer saw the men in Zhukov's party moving across the main deck toward the after brow. He called to Iron Hand on his portable telephone.

"Captain McQuesten, sir, it appears that the Russians have moved to the starboard side quarterdeck and are preparing to embark on a motor launch which is at the foot of the boarding ladder."

Iron Hand acknowledged the message and ordered,

"Surround the area where you see the Russians. Do not fire unless they open up with their weapons first. There are too many civilians walking around the main deck. We will join you immediately."

Iron Hand and Ramsey raced through the passageway but still proceeded carefully enough as they didn't want to run into a rear guard trap. After a few moments they arrived on the main deck and saw Zhukov's party preparing to go down the ladder to the power launch. Iron Hand did a fast count of his men and determined that they and the bad-guys were evenly matched in numbers and fire power.

"All right over there, you men are under arrest! Drop your weapons and raise you hands over your head," Iron Hand shouted.

With Iron Hand's order ringing in their ears, the Russians moved toward the bulkheads, raised their weapons, aimed, and fired at least six shots at Iron Hand and Ramsey. This was their answer to his order. The shots rang out and the bullets ricocheted off the tanker's heavy steel bulkheads behind Iron Hand. Now, with the firing of weapons, the civilian shipboard visitors panicked and began running to take cover. This made any return fire by Iron Hand and his Interpol men impossible. The resulting pandemonium gave Zhukov the opportunity to get his men headed down the ladder to the awaiting power launch. Iron Hand could only wait until the crowd of shipboard visitors left the area.

Zhukov yelled orders to his men to keep firing back at Iron Hand, which they were prepared to do, but three Interpol officers came up from behind and got the drop on them. The two Russians dropped their weapons and raised their hands over their heads.

Bruslov felt out of sorts bringing up the rear of Zhukov's men. The action had ratcheted up and without a weapon he had no way of protecting himself. The men moved through the passageway looking for a ladder to lead them down to the main deck. Shots rang out from behind. Bruslov heard the bullets whiz by his head. He dropped down on the deck passageway and pressed his body against a cleaning gear locker door. The door was unlocked and slowly opened. Bruslov crawled into the locker. Two more shots rang out. He heard someone moan and fall to the deck. Bruslov looked back outside the door and saw one of the briefcases lying on the deck next to the door. He bent down and scooped it up. Two more shots rang out coming from the direction of Zhukov and his men. Bruslov closed the door of the locker and stood in darkness barely breathing for several minutes. He clung to the briefcase that was full of diamonds. His situation was desperate. He heard two or three men run by his hiding place. He decided to remain quiet. After five minutes in the darkness, and hearing no one, he decided to crack open the door and risk looking down the passageway.

He slowly opened the door. One of Zhukov's men was lying wounded on the deck, obviously near death. Bruslov visually checked the passageway in both directions, stepped out of the gear locker, and retreated down the passageway. After a short distance, he came to a ladder leading down to the main deck. He reached the main deck and mixed in with the crowd of visitors who were oblivious to what had been happening on the deck just above them. Bruslov nervously headed toward the quarterdeck and the gangway that would take him off the ship. Bruslov discarded his black jacket and hat. He smiled at the duty officer but made no effort to engage him in conversation. As he walked on to the gangway Bruslov worried for a moment that the duty officer might decided to search the briefcase. Walking down the pier-side gangway the briefcase suddenly seemed much lighter.

Walking down the pier, wild thoughts started to race through his mind now that he had a small fortune in his possession. Should he play it straight and return to Zhukov's headquarters? These diamonds represented more money than he would ever see working for Zhukov. Perhaps he should take the diamonds and run. After all, he had been working for Zhukov for only two days. If he disappeared they wouldn't know where to begin searching for him. No one could ever prove he even had the diamonds. He could just say he decided to quit because he didn't like the shooting and killing. The work was too dangerous. Yes, that was going to be his plan. His personal survival and plans of enrichment kicked into his thought process. He searched for the parked BMW so he could leave the area. He would drive into Marseilles and park the BMW in a garage. He would take a taxi to the train station. His next stop would be Paris.

*   *   *

Iron Hand and Ramsey rushed the after brow deck area. They saw Zhukov and two men each with a briefcase near the bottom platform of the ladder. Iron Hand yelled at the men,

"Stop where you are, Police officers!"

Zhukov yelled to his men,

"Forget them, get into the boat quickly."

Iron Hand fired a shot over the heads of the three men and proceeded to move down the ladder. One of the Russians stopped and took aim at Iron Hand. He fired a shot. It missed, but the bullet ricocheted off the tanker hull and grazed Ramsey's shoulder. Iron Hand returned fire and dropped the Russian on the landing deck platform of the lowered ladder. Zhukov ordered his remaining man to grab the last briefcase and pitch it to him on the power launch.

Iron Hand raced down the remaining steps of the ladder and leaped into the departing power boat. The boat lurched forward and immediately began to pick up speed, moving from the tanker, with Zhukov, a single remaining guard, a previously stationed driver for the boat and Iron Hand on board.

Iron Hand was out numbered three to one but he took on the guard as Zhukov moved to gather up the two briefcases and stow them in the small cabin of the boat. Zhukov was so rattled he had no idea where his new young Russian employee, Bruslov, had gone.

With one swing of his fist, Iron Hand dispatched the first Russian overboard into the wake of the power launch. Now Zhukov began to move toward Iron Hand with a fist clutching a metal club and his pistol in the other hand. Before Iron Hand could fire his weapon the boat took a fast turn to port and both men slipped to the deck. Iron Hand reached out to grab Zhukov's arm to prevent him from swinging the metal club. Both men struggled to gain an advantage. The pilot of the boat was too busy guiding the boat to assist Zhukov. Finally, Iron Hand was able to get the Luger pistol to drop from Zhukov's right hand. Zhukov however, was able to raise himself over Iron Hand and brought his fist down at Iron Hand's head. The blow glanced off the side of his head. Iron Hand rallied and began to struggle with the other arm of Zhukov and his metal club, all the while elbowing Zhukov in his swollen gut. Zhukov reacted by coughing and swearing at Iron Hand as the boat proceeded to gain more speed.

Zhukov seemed to rally and smashed his arm into Iron Hand's body. Iron Hand relaxed his grip on the arm that held the metal club. Zhukov swung the club wildly and hit the boat rail several times as Iron Hand ducked down, avoiding the swinging club. As the boat rocked, Iron Hand swung his leg at Zhukov's lower body and connected. He fell back to the side of the boat. Iron Hand regained his balance, pounced upon Zhukov, bashing him in the back with his large fist causing Zhukov to lose his breath. Iron Hand reloaded his right hand and hit Zhukov in the jaw. He flipped backward and fell overboard. Iron Hand immediately picked up his Beretta and fired a shot at the power boat driver, signaling him to cut power and stop.

As the boat slowed, the driver came back and surrendered to Iron Hand. After securing the boat driver with ropes, Iron Hand looked aft in the boat wake for any sign of Zhukov. Apparently he didn't know how to swim or he sank from exhaustion. In any event the drama was over. In the background he could see a boat speeding to his rescue. Several DST officers waved to him.

Back on the pier, Bruslov stood behind a large stack of boxes and witnessed the demise of Zhukov. He walked further along the pier, past the bow of the tanker where a BMW was parked. He thought perhaps one of Zhukov's men might be in the area, waiting in the darkness for the party of men to return with the diamonds. There were no men standing near the BMW. The SUV's keys were in the ignition. Bruslov climbed in, started the SUV, and looked for a way out of the traffic. He slowly began to drive off the pier.

As Iron Hand waited for his rescue by the DST officers, he reached down and opened up one of the black briefcases that Zhukov had been carrying. He discovered the reason for all the activity: diamonds of every size and quality were packed into the briefcase.

Finally, the DST officers came aboard the power launch and took custody of the remaining man. Zhukov was not recovered from the water; if he had drowned, it could be days before his body would be found. One of the Interpol officers told Iron Hand that Ramsey had been taken to a local hospital for treatment of his bullet wound. Several of the captured Russians admitted to the DST officers that Zhukov had masterminded the entire operation.

Once Iron Hand was back on the pier, he looked around the area for any further sign of the Russians. As he turned his head he noticed a black BMW stuck in traffic as it moving off the pier. The driver appeared familiar. "I've seen that man somewhere," Iron Hand said to himself, as the vehicle slowly moved through the pier traffic.

*   *   *

With the mission completed, Iron Hand turned his thoughts to Goodbody. He reached for his wallet and searched for the telephone number that she had given him. Once more his cell phone worked perfectly. Goodbody answered the telephone.

"Hello."

"How about having a late dinner tonight?" McQuesten's voice caused her to shiver. She didn't keep him waiting for her answer.

"Are you sure that's all, just a late dinner?"

Iron Hand thought to himself, "That's what I like about this Danish woman. She has an imagination."

The Juan les-Pins Affair

Glossary

AMLID: Anti-money laundering International Database.

ASROC: Anti-submarine rocket weapon.

Beretta: Italian hand-gun manufacturer.

Bay of Pigs: Cuban landing site of CIA Cuban militia.

COLA: Cost of living adjustments.

DCI: Director of Central Intelligence.

DDCI: Deputy Director of Central Intelligence.

DGSE: General Directorate for External Security (France)

DST: French Counter-Espionage service.

EBF: European Banking Federation.

ESCB: European System Central Banks.

ETA: Estimated Time of Arrival.

F-8U: LTV supersonic Navy jet fighter of 1960's.

FATF: Financial Action Task Force established by the G-7.

G-7: Group of seven economically developed countries.

INTERPOL: International criminal police organization.

Lugar: German hand-gun manufacturer.

NATO: North Atlantic Treaty Organization.

NOC: Non-official cover-no diplomatic passport; alone.

OFFP: Oil for Food Program sponsored by the UN.

OOD: Officer Of the Deck; who guides the ship.

RPG: Rocket propelled grenade.

SONAR: Sound Navigation and Ranging.